WHO DIES THERE?

WHO DIES THERE?

JAMES DUFF

CUTTING EDGE

ISBN-13: 978-1-962896-01-6

Published by
Cutting Edge Books
PO Box 8212
Calabasas, CA 91372
www.cuttingedgebooks.com

CHAPTER ONE

H E WAS neat to the point of being ridiculous.

He sat opposite me, across the desk, his white-gloved hands folded primly in his lap, staring at nothing in particular out of vacant blue eyes, letting me have my good look at him.

The suit was shantung, light gray, and a red carnation in one lapel matched brightly with red handkerchief, red bow-tie and, I suppose, red socks. The mustache over his thin mouth was tight and blonde, so was his hair; his face, even under the deep tan, appeared a trifle bloated.

All of this, added to the strong odor of rose cologne which wafted away from him with each breath, decided me on one thing. He wasn't the kind of a guy I like to spend my evenings with.

"All right," I said, "now what?"

One white-gloved hand moved down to touch the soft leather of the briefcase near the leg of his chair.

He said: "You are John J. Phelan?"

"That's what the sign on the door says."

He smiled: it was neat and tight and little. He brought the briefcase up into his lap, carefully unzipped it, and took out a large manila envelope. He placed the envelope on the desk between us. His eyes raised to my face.

"I don't suppose," he said, "that you know me?"

"Should I?"

I let the sarcasm push him; he didn't seem to mind it.

"J. Walter Pendleton," he said, breathing a little heavily.

I raised my eyebrows, and shrugged.

"Too bad, Mr. Phelan," he said. He paused "Your reading habits obviously are confined to the lesser things in life."

"My reading habits," I said, "are my business."

"Quite so. Quite so. I don't mean to offend."

His hand caressed the manila envelope. He was getting to me, annoying me; I was making no bones about it.

Traffic tooted around down below on Hollywood Boulevard.

Mr. J. Walter Pendleton cleared his throat uncomfortably and looked over his shoulder, almost as if he expected someone to be sitting there.

"My wife's maiden name, Mr. Phelan, was Baum."

"Well," I said. "Fine."

But I sat up just a little straighter. I have the habit of doing that in the presence of a lot of money. And the name Baum meant more than a lot of money; it meant just about the most.

"That is correct," he said. "My wife is Harry Baum's daughter."

I blinked, and let him see it. Harry Baum had been one of the founding fathers of the never-never land created by the early movie makers. He was long dead, but his name was still spoken in revered tones.

Pendleton smiled. It was a full-grown smile this time, showing a row of even white teeth that appeared real. He glanced at me, and, for one brief second, the blue eyes ceased to be vacant.

"I'm impressed," I said.

"I thought you would be," he said. "Most people are."

He took a lot of time about opening the manila envelope. In fact, he seemed agonizingly slow about everything he did. Finally he removed a sheet of paper from the envelope and dropped it on the desk between us.

I looked at it. It was a glossy print of a photograph. The girl in it was maybe eighteen; certainly no more than that. She was lying on her back on a single bed, staring at the ceiling, so that you only got a profile of her. She was quite nude.

"That," said Pendleton, "arrived last Monday. It came—" he looked away from me "—addressed to my wife."

"Who's the girl?"

"My youngest daughter."

"I see," I said. But I didn't. Not by a long shot.

He took out another photograph and handed it to me.

This time, she was seated on the edge of the bed, her knees tucked tightly up beneath her chin, her arms folded around her shins, her face staring straight into the camera: again she was quite nude.

"That came Tuesday," he said.

"Also addressed to your wife?"

He nodded, and handed me a third photograph. "Wednesday," he said.

Wednesday turned out to be a pose from the rear. The girl was balanced precariously on her toes, looking over her shoulder. She still hadn't put on any clothes.

"Thursday and Friday," he said, handing me the final two photographs.

Thursday she was standing facing the camera, her hands folded in front of her, being quite coy about it all. Friday was a beauty, if you go in for that sort of thing, and I don't.

"I should explain," he said.

"That would be a good idea," I said.

"The girl in the photographs is, as I said, my youngest daughter, Honor. She is, to put it mildly, my wife's favorite. We have two other children, a boy, Joel, and a girl, Landrith. At any rate, my wife has been suffering from a very serious heart condition for the past few years. I think"—and he leaned forward, staring straight at me— "I think that whoever is sending these photographs is trying to shock Mrs. Pendleton to death."

"A nice method of doing it," I said.

I stood up, mainly because I couldn't think of anything else to do at the moment. I walked to the window and looked down at Hollywood Boulevard. Traffic was moving along, as usual. It's one of those streets that never changes: each year brings new faces, but the same hopes. How many kids from how many towns had posed for pictures like those of Honor Pendleton? But there was a difference. She had money. She had background.

I said, without turning: "Has your wife seen these?"

"Of course not." His words bounced against my back.

I turned around to face him. "You want me to find out who is sending them?"

"Of course," he said.

"Uh-huh," I said. "I get fifty a day plus."

"Plus what?"

I had to laugh at that. "Plus expenses."

"That's rather high, isn't it?"

"That's for you to decide, Mr. Pendleton."

He hesitated.

I took out my pipe and began filling it. He made a face.

"Do you have to ?" he asked.

"It's a habit," I said. "Yes."

"I dislike the odor of smoke."

"That's too damned bad. You can buy my time, mister," I said, "but not my habits."

He shuffled his feet against the floor and looked around the office. There wasn't must to see: a desk, three chairs, two file cabinets, a basin and medicine chest in one corner. He wrinkled up his fine little nose in distaste.

I lit my pipe and blew smoke in his direction. The fine little nose wrinkled some more.

"All right," he said.

He reached into his inner coat pocket for a pigskin wallet. He took out a hundred-dollar bill and placed it cautiously on the desk; his fingers were reluctant to leave it. For a guy with, presumably, a couple of hundred million bucks at his disposal, he seemed a bit worried about a mere hundred.

"There," he said.

I didn't touch the bill.

"Okay," I said, "that's good for two days, not counting expenses. I suppose you want me to start immediately?"

He nodded.

"Do you have any ideas, Mr. Pendleton?"

"None," he said. "If I did, I wouldn't be here. A man doesn't like to show around such things to strangers—not when his own daughter is involved."

"How did these photographs arrive?"

"They were in the mailbox each morning, with the regular mail."

"Did you keep the envelopes?"

"No," he said.

"That wasn't very bright," I said.

"I guess not," he said. "But, then, I'm not a detective, Mr. Phelan. I didn't think they would be important."

"Were the envelopes postmarked?"

"No."

"How were they addressed?"

"I told you."

"I mean how. Written in pencil or ink, or typewritten, or how?"

"Oh, that. Well, they were all alike. Printed in ink, addressed to 'Mrs. Sylvia Pendleton.' "

"Was there anything in the envelopes besides the photographs?"

"No—nothing."

"Just how sick is your wife, Mr. Pendleton?"

He looked around the room again. "Quite sick, Mr. Phelan. I guess as sick as one can be and still live."

"May I have the name of your family doctor?"

"Is that necessary?"

"I think it is. Yes."

"Dr. Eugene Margolis, in Beverly Hills."

I picked up the Friday photograph. It made me a little sick.

"Your daughter obviously posed for these pictures of her own will, Mr. Pendleton. Is there any reason to believe she'd like her mother out of the way?"

"I don't like that question, Mr. Phelan."

"Look," I said, "you're hiring me to find out what this is all about. But you've got to cooperate. You've got to tell me what I want to know. You say nothing was in the envelopes but these photographs. Okay. That's a slick way of murdering someone with a weak heart. Shock them to death. It's been done before. But there is the chance that this might just be blackmail. If that's the case, then you or your wife will get another letter or a phone call, demanding money."

"You're not a very trusting person, are you, Mr. Phelan?"

"I can't afford to be. Not in this business."

I moved around the office. I let him think about things for a few minutes, and then I sat down and looked at him.

"There's no reason for Honor to—to want her mother out of the way," he said. "At least, none that I know of. They get along pretty well. I told you—she's her mother's favorite!"

"That's better," I said. "Just what kind of a girl is Honor?"

"Well, she … I don't know, Mr. Phelan. Judging from the photographs, certainly not a very moral one. I guess I haven't been much of a father. I don't understand any of my children, Honor least of all."

He appeared human, for the first time.

"What about your daughter's friends? What kind of people does she run around with?"

He shook his head.

"You do know some of them, don't you?"

"No," he said. "Honor doesn't have anything to do with me. She goes her way, and I go mine. We've sent her to various private schools but for one reason or another she was always asked to leave." He stared at the desk. "I think, Mr. Phelan, that she hates my guts, to be quite frank about it."

"Not much to go on," I said.

He nodded his agreement.

"Let's go back to the envelopes," I said. "Who takes your mail out of the box?"

"The maid. She picks up the letters at about nine each morning and then brings them directly to me."

"Are you in the habit of opening letters addressed to your wife?"

"Since her illness, yes."

"Has your wife any real enemies? By that, I mean anyone who actively hates her?"

"None that I know of. She is, of course, under the handicap of being Harry Baum's daughter. I don't know how much you remember about Harry Baum, Mr. Phelan, but he left not one friend in this world when he passed away. Hollywood, and the whole world for that matter, is quite full of his enemies. He had a knack for cultivating them. I imagine it could be someone left over from my wife's father."

"I doubt that," I said, "but I'll think about it. How about your own enemies, Mr. Pendleton?"

His smile was rather pathetic.

"Mr. Phelan," he said, "as you have probably already judged, I am not one to make much of an impression on people one way or the other. I have no enemies, just as I have no friends."

A peculiar life this guy led.

"Your other two children. Could they have anything to do with this?"

"I really don't know. That's what I'm paying you to find out."

He rose to his feet. He surveyed the crease in his trousers in a mildly impatient manner.

"I'll do what I can," I said. "I'll let you know."

"Please do," he said. He straightened his bow-tie. "Mr. Phelan, perhaps I'm not much of a man by your standards, but my feeling for my wife is sincere. I wouldn't want anything to happen to her. Her life hasn't been too happy."

"I told you," I said. "I'll do what I can."

"That's all I ask."

"You made reference to my reading habits earlier," I said. "What did you mean by that?"

"I'm a poet, Mr. Phelan," he said.

"Oh," I said.

He turned, walking towards the door.

I said: "One other thing, Mr. Pendleton. I suppose there is a will?"

"I suppose there is," he said.

"Any idea who the beneficiary is?"

"I would imagine it's me," he said. "But I'm not sure."

"Okay," I said. "If any more of these photographs show up, make sure you keep the envelopes. It could be important. And, just possibly, if you get a call asking for money, I'd suggest you talk to me first."

He nodded. His glance fell to the five photographs still on the desk.

"Mr. Phelan, I trust—"

"Don't worry about it. I won't show them around."

He smiled, briefly, and left.

I propped up my feet on the desk. I picked up the photographs and went through them again, studying them carefully. Honor Pendleton wasn't a bad-looking dish, if you liked them thin. I didn't. She had all the money in the world and a lot of the looks, but she seemed little different from any Main Street tramp.

The hundred-dollar bill still lay where he had put it. I picked up the phone and dialed a number. The voice on the other end was cautious: "Yes?"

"Eddie, this is Phelan."

"Sure, Johnny. How's it going?"

"I can't complain. How's it with you?"

"I'm getting there, boy, I'm getting there. My ulcer's been giving me holy hell and my old lady's got some stick up her rear about getting a new stove and refrigerator. I can't win."

"You're not supposed to," I said. "Put a hundred on Glory Hole for me in the fourth."

"Ah, Johnny, you're nuts. That's a real dog."

"Just put the bet in the can. It's my money."

"It won't be for long."

I hung up.

Eddie probably was right.

CHAPTER TWO

I had refilled the pipe and had just got it going when she opened the door and stepped into the office.

She looked a lot better with her clothes on than she did without them. Her mouth gave me a bright red slash of a smile and her big brown eyes widened considerably.

"How do you do?" she said.

Just like that.

Her shoulders were rather too wide to be feminine and she was much taller than she had appeared to be in the photographs. She had hair the color of anthracite, cut short like a man's, and skin as white as fresh chalk.

I doubted if she ever saw much of the sun.

She was wearing dark green Bermuda shorts, knee-length lighter green stockings, and a man's white shirt, opened two buttons too low.

She slithered across the office and sat on the edge of the desk. She stuck a cigarette in the red cavern of her mouth and looked at me expectantly.

I didn't move.

"Your manner," she said, "are atrocious."

She lit her own cigarette and blew the smoke in my face.

I had put the photographs back into the manila envelope, but the envelope itself was still lying on top of the desk. She picked it up and started to open it: and then I moved. I grabbed the envelope and put it in the top drawer of the desk.

"Your manners," she said, are still atrocious."

"My mother," I said, "didn't raise me right."

'Whose did?"

I let out a small laugh, and she matched it.

She said: "I was beginning to wonder if you were human."

"Am I?"

"I don't know. Not yet."

"Well," I said, "let's take it up some other time. Right now, I'm busy earning a dishonest dollar."

"You've got big muscles," she said.

"The better to squeeze little girls with."

She stood upright and gave me a harsh look. "I'm not a little girl," she said.

"Run along, angel. You're not my type."

She reached across the desk to slap my face, but I caught her wrist. I almost enjoyed the twist I gave it.

She stepped back and felt her wrist. "You hurt," she said.

"That was my intention."

"I don't think I'm going to like you."

My laugh was a little bigger this time. And this time she didn't match it. She just stood there and looked at me, and there was a lot in the look. She could make a guy uncomfortable.

"What did he want?"

"Who?"

"You know who. Old fusspot."

"I don't know anyone by that name."

"J. Walter Pendleton."

"I don't know anyone by that name, either."

"You annoy me," she said.

"It's a habit I have. I won't apologize for it."

"Did he show you the photographs?"

"Did who show me what photographs?"

"God damn you," she said.

"Look, angel," I said, "it doesn't appear to me that we're evenly matched, so why don't you run along?"

"Whatever he's paying you, I'll double it."

I shook my head. She was a persistent one. I almost liked her; almost, but not quite. Those photographs kept running in front of my eyes. I'm not a moralist, but I put a limit on what goes on, and she had exceeded that limit.

She stood there and I sat there and we let it ride for a while. Finally, she gave out with a big, deep sigh, and settled into the chair opposite me.

"I'm what is usually called a juvenile delinquent," she said.

"You won't get any argument out of me about that."

"You've seen the pictures, then?" She stamped out her cigarette. "Come on, Phelan, level with me. I need someone to level with me."

"You've been going to too many movies," I said.

She was doing pretty good. Maybe someone else would be sucker enough to level with her; but not me, not Phelan. I got over being that big a sucker at the age of eight.

The telephone on the desk jingled. I looked at it, then at her. It continued to jingle. I picked up the receiver.

"John J. Phelan," I said.

"There's a girl in your office." The voice on the other end wasn't much: high-pitched, even behind the obvious handkerchief over the receiver.

"So?" I said.

"So you've also got some pretty pictures of her."

"Go to hell," I said, and slammed down the receiver.

The girl laughed, and said: "You must have loads of friends."

"Thousands," I said.

The phone jingled again. I let it ring four times and then picked it up.

"All right," I said.

"Don't get nasty with me, Phelan." It was the same voice, still pitched too high, still hiding behind the obvious handkerchief.

I said: "I don't do business over the phone."

"You will this time."

The voice on the other end hesitated. The girl got to her feet and came around to sit on the edge of the desk beside me. She had a nice smell about her: not too much, not too little. It bothered me.

"Did her old man show you the pictures?"

"Why?"

She traced a forefinger down my cheek. I slapped her hand away. Her lips moved out into a thin pout: she wasn't used to such treatment.

"I've got the negatives," the voice said, "if you're interested."

"I'm interested."

"I thought you would be."

The lips pouted out a little more. She leaned down, suddenly, and kissed me on the mouth; one hand dug at the buttons on my shirt.

"Just a moment," I said, into the phone.

I put the phone down on the desk, and then stood up. I reached over and slapped her right across the mouth. The imprint of my hand left a dull pink glow on her face. Her eyes opened wide and tears formed in the backs of them and began rolling down her cheeks. I took her by the shoulders and led her around to the other side of the desk and pushed her into the chair there. She bit at her lower lip, much like a child would, and let the tears roll down.

"Sit there," I said, "and have a good cry."

I went back around the desk and picked up the phone again.

"Okay," I said, "how much?"

"Ten thousand."

"That's a lot of money."

"They can afford it."

"I'll talk to my client."

"No. Not to the old man. Don't say anything to him about it. He's so goddamned tight, he wouldn't pay a buck for them. Talk to the kid's older sister, Landrith. She'll play ball. She'll give you the dough."

"Well, well," I said, "that's a new twist."

"Go to the will-call window at the Legion Stadium tonight. There'll be a ticket there for you. Second row, third seat, on the north side. I'll be in the fourth seat. Have the money with you, in cash."

"I'll see what I can do," I said.

"You'd better."

He hung up. I let the phone buzz in my ear for a moment, looking at the girl across from me. She wouldn't return the look.

I hung up. I went over to the basin in the corner. I took a towel and let cold water soak through it, then went back over to her. She didn't resist. I scrubbed her face, washing away all the makeup and the tears. She was a better-looking kid without all the goo. She looked up at me and shook her head.

"I'm not much good," she said.

"Don't let it get you down," I said. "You're young."

"Maybe," she said. "That doesn't excuse anything. That's what they all do, excuse me because I'm young."

"How old are you?"

"A hundred and eight," she said.

"Okay. You'd better run along."

"Of course." She hesitated. "I sure have a knack for causing everyone trouble." She tried to smile, but it didn't come off. "Oh, well."

She got up and walked to the door. She stopped there, turning back to look at me.

"That's the first time anyone's ever slapped me," she said.

"Like I said, you're young."

"Like I said, maybe."

"Look, angel, don't feel too sorry for yourself. That's the wrong pitch."

She nodded, and closed the door behind her.

Sometimes, in this business, you act like a heel. Sometimes, the act goes out the window and you really are a heel. Sometimes it's just a lousy, stinking way of making a living.

I opened the bottom desk drawer and took out a bottle of Four Roses. I took a long slug of it.

It didn't help much.

It never does.

I looked up Dr. Eugene Margolis in Beverly Hills. He had a Crestview number, and I dialed it. The nurse that answered told me that Dr. Margolis was on hospital call that afternoon and would not be in. I asked for his home number. She asked me why I wanted it. I told her I didn't feel so hot. She offered to give me another doctor's number or have Dr. Margolis call me later.

A sweet nurse, that one.

I looked up J. Walter Pendleton. He had a listing in San Fernando Valley, in that section where only the elite of the movie world live—in $250,000 houses. I dialed his number. The voice that answered was sugary.

"Hello," the voice said. "Pendleton residence."

"I'd like to speak to Mr. Pendleton, please."

"Which one?"

"The old one, honey. J. Walter."

The sugar became laughter. "You must be that private detective fellow he went to see. Mr. Phelan. Is that right?"

"You get around. Who's this?"

"I'm Mabel, the maid."

"Sounds like a song."

She coughed lightly and said: "Just a moment, please."

The tone of her voice had changed. I could hear her talking in the background, but could not quite make out the words. Another voice said something quite sharply to her, and I recognized it. There was a pause, and then J. Walter Pendleton himself said: "Hello?"

"This is Phelan."

"Yes?" He didn't sound very pleased at hearing from me.

"That's a nice maid you've got. Does she know everything that goes on around there?"

"She has the usual female habit of sticking her nose into where she's not wanted, Mr. Phelan. She's been with my wife since the beginning of time and, unfortunately, seems to think she's a permanent fixture around here."

"And she isn't?"

"Mr. Phelan, I didn't hire you to discuss my servant problem. What is it you want?"

"A man called me a short while ago. He told me he had the negatives of those photographs. He wants $10,000 for them."

It was awfully quiet on the other end of the line.

"Are you there, Mr. Pendleton?"

"That's a lot of money," he said.

"That's what I told him."

Again he was silent. I waited, and then waited some more, and then I said: "A funny thing, Mr. Pendleton. He wanted me to ask your other daughter, Landrith, for the money and not you."

"I'm pleased that you told me," he said.

"I'm Working for you. Remember?"

"Quite so," he said. He hesitated. "When does he want the money?"

"Tonight," I said. "He's reserved a seat for me at the fights. I'm to meet him there."

"I suggest you do meet him, Mr. Phelan, and discuss the situation with him."

I didn't see that there was a hell of a lot to discuss.

"Without the money?"

"Without the money," he said.

"You're the boss."

"You don't approve?"

"No, I don't, Mr. Pendleton. But then I'm only a poor slob trying to keep ahead of his bookie. It's not my wife."

"Please allow me to worry about Mrs. Pendleton," he said. "Besides, it now appears to be a simple case of blackmail, and not attempted murder."

Blackmail usually led to murder: at least in my experiences. But I didn't tell him that.

"Okay," I said.

"Try and stall for time, Mr. Phelan. Maybe we can put an end to this sordid business. I'll leave it to your judgment about how to do so. I feel sure that you've run up against similar situations many times in your business."

I was glad he was sure.

I told him I'd call him later that night with the news, and he hung up. But the phone didn't go dead. I smiled, and said: "Did you get all of it, Mabel?"

There was a slight chuckle from the other end of the line, and then the click of a line gone dead.

I sat there in the office and listened to the traffic noises down on Hollywood Boulevard and felt the hot air coming in on my back and thought of a lot of nice things that I'd thought of when I was a kid and I wondered what in hell had happened to all those nice things.

It was a great life.

I took out the bottle and had another slug.

It still didn't help much.

I took out the photographs and gave them another once-over. I was getting to know them pretty much by heart. She had a nice clean-looking body, and a pert little smile. Too bad. What made a kid with her background do such things? I couldn't figure it.

I looked at Friday's photo a long time. The guy in it had a real sweet face; yeah, a real sweet face.

I wondered if he'd be the guy I'd be seeing that night.

There was only one way to find out.

CHAPTER THREE

THE LEGION STADIUM is Hollywood's ivory tower of violence. There's a boxing card there every Saturday night of the year. The place is located only a few blocks from the fabled but saddening intersection of Hollywood and Vine. It has the strangest clientele of any boxing stadium in the country. The balconies are filled weekly with the Mexican kids from the lower east side, yelling in the strange jabber of half-English, half-Spanish that passes for a language, cheering on their favorites much as their parents and their grandparents had cheered on favorite matadors in the past. The main floor is a strange conglomeration. Big-shouldered, big-bellied movie stars, some on the way up, some on the way down, but all letting the fans have a look at them, letting the fans know they're good "sports." Big-hipped, big-lipped, big-breasted females, the semipros in the art of love, on the prowl for a big name or a big anything, it doesn't really matter. The place is also full of shifty-eyed gamblers, running here and there, listening to the talk, watching the odds, trying to get in on a "fix," sucking their proverbial cigar butts, looking the way a cinema conception of a gambler should look; of tourists, doing what tourists all over the world are doing at any and all times, looking for a cheap thrill, a name, a place, anything to build up and tell the folks back home. A few died-in-the-wool fight fans are mingled in with the rest. They sit there among the noises and the smells, strangely quiet throughout it all, going over each punch and counterpunch, each feint, each thumb in the eye, each elbow in the Adam's apple, each knee in the crotch, remembering other fighters from other years, always remembering, always haggling within themselves: this is the Legion Stadium.

I had taken the manila envelope with its precious photographs to the Hollywood bus terminal and deposited it in one of those rental boxes. After that, I had had dinner at Mike Lyman's, then gone to my apartment for a brief nap. So it was late when I got to the Legion; there wasn't much of a crowd left on the outside, just a few guys milling around, doing nothing, wanting nothing.

The fellow behind the will-call window handed me a white envelope—with my name scrawled on the outside. Inside, was a ticket on the north side, row B, seat three. Second row, third seat.

I asked the clerk if there was any way of my finding out who had left the ticket for me. He looked at me, laughed slightly, and hunched up his shoulders.

That was all the answer I could get out of him.

It smelled inside, the way it always smells in any fight stadium: a smell of stale tobacco and stale bodies, and the faint, peculiar smell of people watching a couple of dough-heads beat the hell out of each other.

I stood on the ramp on the north side and watched the six-round semi-windup between a bald-headed old geezer with an inner-tube around his middle and a sleek young colored boy with a quick right hand and nothing much else.

The house was full. It was also disgusted with the two guys in the ring. The colored boy would dance around on his toes, paw awkwardly with his left, and then throw his right, and then the old geezer would tie him up in knots and the waltz would continue. It was pretty sad. The constant pounding of feet against floor started and got so bad that you couldn't hear yourself think.

I gave my ticket to an usher and he led me down the aisle to my seat.

The fourth seat was empty.

The guy on my left, in the second seat, was a beauty, though. He was about five-feet-two with eyes-of-blue and a fat paunch that hung out over the edge of his seat, and, it seemed, a deep hatred for anything that wasn't pure white. I stepped on his feet getting into my seat and he looked up at me with those blue eyes and said, "Chrissakes, watch it, will ya?" and I murmured, "Sorry."

The main event was between Luis "Lulu" Sanchez, a popular young Mexican kid from the east side, and Kid Frisco. God only knew where Kid Frisco was from, or how old he was. He turned out to be a squat little Italian with a battered face and a bored manner from having gone through the routine too many times; he didn't get much of a hand, but Blue-Eyes next to me damned near had apoplexy cheering for him.

When Sanchez came down the aisle towards the ring, I thought the place would break apart. It was mass hysteria. He was a clean-looking kid, just past twenty, neat and trim. He wore his black hair in a crew-cut, and he kept jiggling his feet all the way down the aisle and waving and laughing at the crowd: he was the picture of self-confidence. When he reached the aisle opposite me, he paused, turning to look at me. He smiled at me, a big smile, and winked.

I didn't get it: not then.

I sat there through the first four rounds, and nothing much happened, either in the ring or out of it, except that Blue-Eyes was having himself a form of enjoyment; he kept yelling, "Kill that Mex! Kill him, Kid! Kill him!" This was a real nice egg, this Blue-Eyes.

It was a mismatch from the opening bell. Sanchez knew it, Kid Frisco knew it, the crowd knew it, and Sanchez knew that the crowd knew it. The Mexican kid kept dancing around Kid Frisco, playing with him, jabbing with his left, jabbing, jabbing, jabbing, never getting in close. Everyone seemed happy about the whole thing but Kid Frisco and Blue-Eyes. And me, possibly; I was getting a little anxious.

As the bell rang to end round four and Kid Frisco waddled back to his corner, Sanchez leaned over the edge of the ropes and again looked at me: only this time, he didn't smile. Seat four was still vacant.

But it wasn't for long.

I don't know what I had expected, but what came certainly wasn't it.

Adam Wheeler was a detective-lieutenant in Homicide. He was tall and angular, and he was also one of the smartest cops I'd ever met, and I've met a lot of them, believe me. He settled into the fourth seat, pulled out a stick of chewing gum, folded it in half, then in half again, then stuck it in his mouth.

"How you doing, Johnny?" he asked.

"It's a lousy fight," I said.

"Figures," he said. "The Mexican kid's getting the build-up for a trip back east."

Round five had started. Sanchez was watching Wheeler more than he was Kid Frisco. The fighter's face was puzzled.

"Let's go outside and talk, Johnny," Wheeler said.

"About what?"

"We'll think up something."

"I want to watch the fight."

"It won't surprise you any," he said. "Let's go."

I hesitated a moment, and then said: "I never argue with a cop from Homicide."

Wheeler's angular face turned in my direction. "The hell you yell."

We walked up the aisle and then outside. Blue-Eyes seemed saddened at my departure. He was a guy I would remember.

It was a cool night for that time of year. The neon lights from Hollywood Boulevard glowed dully against the dark sky. A slight breeze riffled through the tall oak trees lining the street, and I could hear Wheeler's mouth moving over his gum.

"Okay, Adam," I said, "here we are."

He started a smile, then held it back.

"Mind coming downtown with me?" he asked.

"Depends."

"On what?"

"I'd like to know what it's all about," I said.

"You'll find out," he said.

"You're sure as hell a talkative bastard," I said.

He let the smile come on full this time.

"Come on, Johnny. I'm a cop, making my four hundred and change a month. Don't give me a bad time."

"Okay, okay," I said. "Don't give me the sob story. I'll go with you, but just because I don't have anything better to do."

He didn't even thank me.

We rode downtown in a squad car with a uniformed cop for a driver. We didn't say much on the way down. I asked about his wife and kids and he said they were fine and they wanted to know when I was coming out to dinner again. It was that way between Adam and me. We'd spent a lot of time together in the mud: Saint Lo, Aachen, the Ardennes; yeah, a lot of time.

We went up to the third floor and through a small, dingy office with a couple of uniformed cops and a fat old Mexican woman sobbing out her heart in it, and back to a larger, but still dingy, office.

There was only one man in the room: Chief of Detectives Dan Lundeberg. I've never yet looked at him without getting that tight little knot in the middle of my stomach. He's that kind of a guy.

He was big and blonde, a slat-bodied Swede with colorless eyes hiding behind rimless glasses, and a habit of wanting and getting his own way.

"Jesus Christ," he said, "you again?"

I smiled, just for his benefit, but his face didn't change; it never did.

"I swear I'm innocent," I said, still smiling.

"Of what?" Lundeberg asked.

"Of whatever it is you get in mind," I said.

"Jesus Christ," he said again, and grunted. He looked at Wheeler. "He was in that seat?"

"He was," said Wheeler.

"You got a habit, Phelan," said Lundeberg, "of being in the wrong place at the right time."

Wheeler pushed a chair up behind me, and I sat down. Lundeberg took a lot of time lighting a cigarette, and then he leaned back and stared at the ceiling. He made a smacking noise with his lips and shook his head.

"You a fight fan, Phelan?" he asked.

"On occasion."

"Like tonight, huh?"

"Like tonight," I said.

"Uh-huh," he said. "When was the last time you went to the fights?"

"That's my business."

He smacked his lips again, and looked at Wheeler. "You tell him anything?"

Wheeler shook his head.

Lundeberg swung his gaze back to me. "Then why you acting dumb, Phelan?"

"It's just my way," I said.

Lundeberg said: "You also got a habit, Phelan, of irritating the hell out of me."

My smile grew another inch.

"You'd make a good cop, Phelan," Lundeberg said. "A damned good cop. We could use smart guys like you in the department." He looked at Wheeler, then back at me again. "I don't know what kick you get out of being a private dick. Trouble with you private dicks is that you've all seen too many movies. You got stock answers, stock smart-guy attitudes. I don't mind, not as long as you don't interfere with my business. You want to tail some broad cheating on her ever-loving, that's okay. It's none of my business. But you, Phelan, you're a little different from the rest. You continually stick your nose in my business. That, I don't like."

I let the smile leave my face, and stood up. I let him see that I was a little mad; just a little, not too much.

"Look, cop," I said, "you're wasting my time: I came down here as a favor to Wheeler there. I haven't got any idea what's eating you, and you're beginning to bore me. If you've got anything you want to ask me, ask it and be damned quick about it. I don't like the stink in here."

The colorless eyes swept over my face and, for one brief second, I thought I saw something change in the backs of them. But maybe it was only my imagination.

Lundeberg opened the top drawer in the desk, took out a sheet of paper, and handed it to me. It was a photograph. I was getting pretty good at looking at them. The guy in the photograph was lying on his back, his left arm stretched out on a heavily flowered carpet, his right crossed over his stomach, his eyes staring upwards at the camera in that way the dead have of staring; there were a couple of little holes in the front of his shirt and dark spots around the holes.

He was as dead as anyone I'd ever seen.

I looked at his face and the back of my head began to ache and it was all I could do to keep a straight face.

"Nice-looking kid," I said.

"Ever see him before?" asked Lundeberg.

"Never."

But I had. The only other time had also been in a photograph. He hadn't had any clothes on that time, though.

"That's funny," said Lundeberg.

"Yeah," I said. "I get my kicks out of looking at stiffs."

Wheeler moved around in front of me. He sat on the edge of the desk and swung one leg back and forth.

Wheeler said: "We thought you might know him."

"Well, think again. I don't."

"That's funny," said Lundeberg.

"You're in a rut," I said. "It's a riot."

Lundeberg stretched his arms wearily in the air. He was tired. He was doing a job, and that's all it was to him: a job. He took a lot of time with another cigarette. Wheeler kept swinging his leg back and forth, back and forth.

This could get monotonous: it was getting monotonous.

"Well," I said, "if that's all, I'll be going."

"This guy," said Lundeberg, ignoring my comment, "was found at seven twenty-two this evening in his apartment on the Sunset Strip. Those two holes came from a .38. On a table near his phone was a pad. On the pad was written, 'north side, second row, seats three and four'."

"Oh?" I said.

"You were sitting in seat three, Johnny," said Wheeler.

"What does that make me?"

"Where were you earlier this evening?" asked Lundeberg.

"I haven't the slightest goddamned idea," I said. I walked to the door, then paused. "What the hell's the matter with you, Lundeberg? You've been at this job too long. You're slipping. There's a dozen places in Los Angeles that could mean north side, second row, seats three and four. You're wasting my time, and it's too valuable to waste."

"Maybe," said Lundeberg. "Maybe."

I said: "What was the stiff's name?"

"Why do you want to know?" asked Lundeberg. "There's no connection between you. It doesn't interest you."

"No," I said. "it doesn't."

"Some day, Phelan," said Lundeberg, "you're going to get too damned smart with me. I'm going to tie you up in little knots and feed you to the fishes when that day comes."

"Don't hold your breath," I said.

I opened the door and started to leave.

"His name was Sanchez," said Lundeberg. "Memo Sanchez."

Goddamn, I thought. That was all. Goddamn.

It was a little after midnight when I got to my apartment. I unlocked the door and stepped inside and switched on the overhead light.

There were two of them. One was sitting in the easy chair, a funny little grin on his wide, fattish, Maxican face. He was holding a shiny black .38 right on my middle. The other one moved away from the wall. He was short and thin, about featherweight, with a crinkled pinkish scar beneath his left eye.

He hit me right in the stomach with his left fist.

It hurt. I doubled over, and he brought his right around, catching me on the point of the chin. I fell to the floor and things started to blacken a bit. I tried to catch his shoe coming at my face, but I was too slow.

The guy kept hitting me, and hitting me some more. He used his fist on my face and midsection, and his knee on my groin. He would grunt each time he hit me, and the other guy in the chair would laugh.

The last thing I remember was him hitting me.

They sure as hell enjoyed themselves.

CHAPTER FOUR

I NEVER did like the taste of wool. My mouth was pushed into the rug and there wasn't a bone or a muscle in my body that wasn't crying out in pain. Something kept ringing and ringing and ringing in my ears. I pushed myself up into a sitting position and tried to look around.

I was still in the same world.

I felt my head: it was still there.

I felt my ribs: none of them had been broken.

And then I got the taste of blood along with the wool.

And that something kept ringing and ringing and ringing.

I got to my feet. It took a lot out of me, but I made it. I stumbled against a chair getting to the door, and had to fight my way to my feet again. I finally made the door, and opened it. I tried to focus on whatever it was out there, but the blur wouldn't go away.

I was slipping again. I slipped a long way.

This time, I wasn't so sure I was in the same world.

I was drifting along on a soft, billowy cloud. Music was coming from nowhere, helping me along. A brown-eyed angel stood over me, her hand cool and pleasant on my forehead. I pulled the hand down to my lips and kissed it. It felt real.

The hand pulled itself away from me, and the brown-eyed angel gave me an unkind look and moved out of my sight.

I sat up.

The soft, billowy cloud turned out to be my own bed. The music was coming from my portable radio on the dresser. The brown-eyed angel was human, after all—too human.

She was tall, and her skin was darker than her sister's, as if she spent some time in the sun, and her hair was a trifle lighter; she was as beautiful as anything I'd ever seen, and she knew it.

"Hello," she said.

"Is that all?" The sound of my own voice surprised me.

She nodded, and started moving around the room. She was wearing a light tan skirt and a darker tan sweater that made no attempt to hide her obvious charms: it would have failed anyway. She was wearing low-heeled shoes.

"You with them?"

She didn't answer. She ignored me. She kept opening drawers and doors, poking through everything, obviously looking for something.

I didn't have to be told what it was.

I felt my body, and discovered that I was stripped down to my shorts. My groin had a dull, constant throb in it, and there were a few ugly welts across my chest and stomach.

Those boys had known what it was all about. They'd done a good job.

I tried to get out of bed. She came quickly across the room. Her hands were strong on my shoulders, pushing me back into bed.

"Where do you think you're going?" she asked.

Her voice, I noticed for the first time, had a lilting, musical quality about it.

"I want to get up."

She laughed, and said: "Oh, my God."

"I'm a comic, I am," I said.

"You will be," she said, "if you try to get out of that bed."

"You didn't answer my question."

"What question?"

"Are you with them?"

"Oh, don't be a silly ass," she said.

It was a little too late for that.

I lay there, and watched her finish her search of the room. She apparently had gone through the other rooms while I was out cold. Finally, she shrugged, and gave up. She came over and sat down on the edge of the bed. She lit two cigarettes and handed me one. The smoke burned my insides.

"What time is it?"

She looked at her watch. "Ten after three."

"What day?"

"Sunday morning."

"What month and year?"

She laughed again. It was the kind of laugh you like to hear, the kind that sort of grows on you.

The music stopped, and some guy began chanting about the merits of buying a used car from Uncle Andy. She got up and turned off the radio.

"Did you bring me in here?"

"I did," she said. "You're pretty heavy, mister."

"I guess I should thank you," I said.

"That would be nice."

"Thanks."

"You're welcome." She studied the tips of her fingers; there was no polish on them. "You were in pretty rotten shape. Does that happen often?"

"Occupational hazard," I said. "Have you got a mirror?"

"Why?"

"I'd like to look at my face. I'd like to find out if I'm still handsome."

"That can wait. Where are the photographs?"

"What photographs?"

She made a face, and shook her head.

I said: "Are you in the habit of calling on men this time of night?"

"When I want something, I am. I want something now." She laughed again. "Besides, you're in no condition to bother me."

"I'm afraid I just can't help you in any way."

"I was hoping you'd be more cooperative."

"You're Landrith Pendleton," I said.

"My, my," she said, "aren't we getting bright?"

I stubbed out my cigarette in the bedside ashtray. I smoke cigarettes if I have to, but I'm really a pipe man. The phone began ringing in the front room. She stood up.

"Want me to answer it?" she asked.

I shook my head. "It's not important. Nothing's important at three o'clock in the morning."

"Some day," she said, "I'll have to show you just how wrong you are."

The phone gave up. She sat back down.

"I'd like to have those photographs, Mr. Phelan," she said. Her voice had lowered one octave.

She stubbed out her own cigarette, and sat staring at her calm hands. She raised those big brown eyes to look at me one time, and then lowered them again. This one could be a lot of trouble. Where Honor Pendleton was a girl, this one was a women. Where Honor threw her sex at you, almost forcing it on you, this one held it back, letting you know it was hard to get, but still there. Landrith was much more dangerous; she was slow-burning, but I'd hate to be around her when the fire really got going—or maybe I wouldn't.

"Those photographs wouldn't do you any good, angel," I said. "The negatives would still be out somewhere."

"I'll climb that hill when I get to it."

"Have you seen them?"

She hesitated, then shook her head.

"The guy that was in one of them," I said, "was killed tonight. They found him in his apartment with a couple of .38 slugs in him. It wasn't pretty."

She wrung her hands together, but her face didn't change.

"I had the photographs," I said, "but I doubt if they're still around. Those pants you took off me"—she turned her head away; I thought I caught the faint beginnings of a blush—"go look in them. See if there's a key in the right front pocket."

She got up and went over to the chair where she had put my pants. She went through all the pockets. The key wasn't in them.

"I didn't think it would be there," I said.

"Is that why they beat you up?"

"I suppose so. I can't think of any other reason."

Her shoulders sagged. "Honor is such a ... " She looked at me, and didn't finish.

"Do you know anybody named Sanchez?"

Something moved across her face, but it didn't come out. She shook her head and moved towards the door.

"Good night, Miss Pendleton," I said. "Thanks again."

She turned in the doorway. "My friends call me Lannie."

"I'll remember that. Good night, Lannie."

"I didn't say we were friends yet. I'll think about it."

"You do that," I said.

"I'll do that," she repeated. "We'll meet again."

"Sure," I said.

She gave me a weak smile and then left.

I heard the front door close behind her. I rolled over on my side and turned out the light. The darkness was welcome. The Pendletons were quite a family. So far. For fifty bucks a day plus I was sure getting in deep. I didn't much like it. No, I didn't.

I kept thinking of that sixth photograph I'd seen, of the way the guy had been lain out on the floor: and I also kept thinking of those two muggs, the one grunting as he was hitting me, and the other one laughing.

I'd like to meet them again some day.

Yeah, I would.

I slept on that.

CHAPTER FIVE

S UNDAY MORNING. I got up and hobbled into the kitchen and
put on the coffee pot and then went into the bathroom. My
face was a good advertisement on how-not-to-get-along-in-the-
world. My left eye had a beautiful purplish-gold mouse beneath
it; there was an inch-long gash across my forehead, and another
one slightly longer running down from the corner of my right
eye on to my cheekbone.

Otherwise, I was in great shape.

I went back into the kitchen and drank two quick cups of
coffee, and then I got the Sunday *Times* from the front door. I
nursed along a third cup of coffee laced with a shot of brandy
while reading the news. There was a four-paragraph story about
the murder of Memo Sanchez on Page 2. It referred to him as
being the older brother of Luis "Lulu" Sanchez, popular local
welterweight. Lulu had won his 22nd straight fight the night
before at the Legion, a technical knockout over Kid Frisco in the
seventh round.

Apparently, I thought, he had gotten tired of playing around
with the little Italian after I had left.

Memo Sanchez had been a war hero: Distinguished Service
Cross and Purple Heart in Korea. But he was known to have been
quite a gambler, and the police were theorizing that his death had
been brought about by his betting habits.

I turned to the sports page. There was a picture of Lulu in
his dressing room after the fight. He had not been informed of

his brother's death until after the knockout. His face was blank; nothing showed on it.

I looked at the race results. Glory Hole had finished seventh in a nine-horse field at Santa Anita.

Oh, well. Oh, hell.

I showered and made a half-hearted attempt at shaving over the bumps and bruises. I stopped down at the corner drugstore and had another cup of coffee and two fried eggs. The eggs did a lot of things to my stomach they shouldn't have done.

I drove out Hollywood Boulevard to the corner of Baker. I parked near there, and then walked back to the cigar store on the corner.

The little round guy behind the counter had a yellow pencil resting behind one ear and a self-satisfied grin on his round face. He needed a shave and he smelled like a bottle of stale beer. The self-satisfied grin went away as he looked up at me.

"Eddie," I said.

He shook his head, and said: "You'd better change your way of living, Johnny. You don't look so good."

"I don't feel any better than I look."

"What happened?"

"I got mixed up with Snow White and the Seven Dwarfs."

He didn't laugh.

I took out my wallet, and carefully separated the hundred-dollar bill from among the several ones there. I looked at the clock on the wall: it was twelve-fifteen. I hadn't even had the thing twenty-four hours yet. I handed the bill to Eddie. He looked at it, fingered it, then put it away under the counter.

"I told you, sucker," he said.

"You know a guy named Memo Sanchez?" I asked.

His face grew wary. "Heard of him."

"Heard what?"

"He got bumped last night." He looked out of the store at a high-heeled blonde clicking her way up the street. "He wasn't a bad kid. Not really. A little on the flashy side, you know, like most of these Mexicans. But not a bad kid. He just reached for the wrong star."

"What star would that be?"

"Come on now, Johnny," he said. "We been friends a long time. I'm in business. You know I can't answer that."

"Who's running the books in this end of town now?"

Eddie shook his head.

"Thanks," I said, turning to leave.

"Johnny," he said, "I hear tell there's a joker in the third at Caliente this afternoon. Want on him?"

"How much of a joker is he?"

He spread his hands. "All the way."

"It'll come out of your pocket," I said.

"No," he said. "Not mine. I'm just working here."

"Thanks anyway, Eddie," I said. "I don't trust jokers."

"You're a hard guy to figure, Johnny. But I like you. Don't ask me why, but I do." He smiled, then pursed up his lips. "Ever hear of a guy named Richie Egan?"

"Sure. Runs the Red Barn across the county line in Ventura."

"Uh-huh," said Eddie. "That's him. Real nice guy. Real nice place, that Red Barn. But don't stick your nose in too far, Johnny. I hear he's only nice up to a certain point."

"Thanks again, friend," I said.

It took me forty minutes to drive out to Hidden Oaks in the San Fernando Valley. Hidden Oaks is a quaint little place, at the west end of the valley. As the name implies, it is hidden among a lot of oak trees in the only cool spot in the whole valley. It's where the real elite live. No fly-by-night glamor boys; no screwy front-page names. Just the people with the money behind the movies, and maybe a few real big-time actors and directors thrown in for atmosphere.

The Pendleton estate was a huge colonial mansion with a rolling green front lawn the size of a golf course. I drove through a grove of oak trees and along the cool greenness of the lawn up to the house, surprised at the lack of a guard. I parked the Dodge behind a block-long black Caddie and walked up to the front door.

The guy that answered my ring had stepped right out of the movies. He was veddy, veddy English, dressed in a butler's get-up, and with a bored, disinterested look on his face. He took one look at my battered puss, and his nose went straight up in the air.

"Is Mr. Pendleton in?" I asked.

The disinterest increased. "Which one?"

"Mr. J. Walter Pendleton," I said.

The nose climbed another inch. "He never sees anyone on Sunday afternoon."

"Well," I said, "let's make an exception this one time. You run along now like a good little boy and tell him John J. Phelan is here, biting at the bit."

"I am sorry," he said.

He started to close the door in my face. I wedged my foot in the door and placed a hand on his chest, and pushed just a bit. It shocked him half to death.

He looked down at my hand on his chest, then turned around and disappeared. I had the idea he was going to change clothes.

I stepped inside the door and waited. I was in a small alcove, guarded on either side by a ten-foot high marble statue. The one on the left was male: he was wearing a fig leaf; his arms were lowered towards his knees, and his head was bowed. The statue on the right was female: she wasn't wearing anything; her arms were stretched towards the sky, and her head was looking in the same direction as her arms.

I supposed it was symbolic, or something.

Presently, the butler returned. He maintained a respectful distance and said, "This way, please," and I followed him out of the alcove into a large room with a bare floor and Louis XIV furnishings and miles of tapestries hanging all over the place, and then into a hallway and down that for a few dozen miles, past four doors. We finally stopped in front of a door that was painted white except for a blue star the size of a quarter right in the middle of it.

The butler knocked hesitantly, then opened the door and stepped aside. I went in, and he closed the door after me.

The room was about twenty-five feet square. It was painted a stark white, like the door and, on each wall and on the ceiling, were duplicates of the blue star on the door. There were no windows in the room and only one piece of furniture: a faded white wooden kitchen stool about four-feet high upon which perched Mr. J. Walter Pendleton with a pad and pencil in his hands. He was wearing a tuxedo, a T-shirt, and a top hat.

I laughed, and he frowned.

"Please be so kind as to keep your laughter to yourself, Mr. Phelan, and don't be so quick to judge me as an idiot. This happens to be the only way in which I can create." His glance narrowed on my face. "Good heavens, man, what happened to you?"

"A couple of guys wanted those pictures you left with me."

"Did they get them?"

"That they did."

He shook his head. I stood there and looked around. There wasn't much to see.

"I'd offer you a chair"—he smiled a vacant little smile—"except, of course, you will not be staying long and there isn't one anyway."

I could see that.

"Did you talk to that man last night?"

"What makes you think it was a man?"

"You said as much, didn't you?"

"I guess I did. No, I didn't talk to him."

"And why not?"

"He didn't show up."

He grunted. "Probably frightened away at the last moment. I, of course, haven't had your experience in these matters, Mr. Phelan, but I imagine that blackmailers are a pretty disgusting lot."

"This one also happens to be quite dead, Mr. Pendleton," I said. "If that's what he was, a blackmailer."

He didn't move for a full thirty seconds. Then, he carefully stepped down from his perch on the stool, placed pad and pencil on the seat, and then turned to me.

"Dead," he said. "Dead, did you say, Mr. Phelan?"

"That's what I said."

"Well, well," he said, and the thing that was on his face might have been a smile. "That seems to take care of our problem, doesn't it?"

"I don't think so."

"Oh? And why not?"

"Whoever murdered him now has the negatives. I don't think the police found them, but I'm not sure. Call it a hunch, if you want, but I'm sure those negatives are floating around somewhere. And there's also the possibility that it was a different party that took the photographs away from me last night."

"I see. You're quite right."

He began walking around the room. He reminded me of an animal in the zoo, impatiently pacing back and forth within the strict confines of his cage.

"Well, well," he said again. "Who was the murdered man, Mr. Phelan?"

"His name was Memo Sanchez. He was a fast-living Mexican kid, out of his element on the Sunset Strip."

"Memo Sanchez." He sort of purred over the name. "Do the police have any clues as to the murderer?"

"They don't confide in me, but I would imagine not. They were shooting in the dark when they had me down at the station last night."

He gave me a startled look. "The Pendleton name didn't come up, did it?"

I shook my head.

He sighed. "Frankly, Mr. Phelan, I'm at a loss as to what to do next."

I said, "If the police do have those negatives, Mr. Pendleton, which I doubt, it won't take them long to identify your daughter. They have the ways and the means. And then she'd be the prime suspect. I've got a personal grudge in this thing now. I'd like to keep on it. Those two birds that worked me over last night have got something coming to them."

"All right," he said, "you just go ahead, Mr. Phelan."

I hesitated, then: "Your hundred bucks has run out."

He frowned, then dug in his pocket. The bill he handed me was another hundred-dollar one: that seemed to be all he ever carried.

"Will that do, Mr. Phelan?"

"It will," I said, "for now."

"If you run into the police again, please be discreet."

"Don't worry," I said.

"And now, Mr. Phelan, if you don't mind—" He looked at the door.

"Okay," I said. "I'll keep in touch."

I turned and left the room.

The air in the hallway was much better. At least, there was air. I stood in the hallway and thought about the Pendletons I had met: one sex-starved little tramp, one half-cracked poet, and one beautiful thing I hadn't as yet figured out. Quite a family. I wondered just how good a poet J. Walter was. I made a mental note to check on it; I wanted him to be a lousy one. I don't know, I just did.

I started back down the long hallway, but I didn't get past the second door. The woman who stood in the doorway was big and solid and the color of rich chocolate; she was wearing a loose-fitting housecoat, a permanent smile, and an ageless face.

"Come in, Mr. Phelan," she said, "Mrs. Pendleton would like to see you."

"You," I said, "could only be Mabel."

She said: "Mabel, the maid. You know, sounds like a song."

"You've got big ears, Mabel."

"Can't help that. It's just my way."

She laughed. It came from somewhere deep within her and sort of boomed out into the hallway and bounced around between the walls.

I followed her into the room. It was sunny and yet quite cool without the aid of air conditioning. The furnishings were nice and neat and feminine. A few watercolors dotted the walls; they were all landscapes and farm houses, and they weren't much good.

The woman sitting in the wicker rocker turned to look at me. The wide expanse of the picture window overlooking the rolling lawn made a nice backdrop for her. Her skin was almost thin enough to be transparent, but her eyes were what caught and held me: they were big and brown, like her daughter's; as big and brown as anything I'd ever seen.

She had a thin Indian blanket wrapped around her legs. She picked at the edge of the blanket and continued to look at me.

"Well, Mr. Phelan," she said in a thin, waspish voice. "I understand you've just had a privileged visit to the inner sanctum."

"If that's what you call it," I said, and added: "It's quite a room."

"My husband fancies himself a genius, Mr. Phelan, and, as such, thinks certain eccentricities become him." She turned to Mabel. "Iced tea for our guest, please, Mabel." She nodded at a chair beside her, and I sat down. "Unfortunately, Walter falls quite a few degrees lower than being a genius. However, each man has at least one vice—women, drink, gambling, whatever.

Each man has his own. I can't complain. With Walter, it just happens to be sitting in that god-awful room and staring at those blue stars and, as he calls it, creating."

"Is he any good?"

"That is a difficult question to answer, Mr. Phelan. I'll reply, though, in this way: the critics, in the beginning, thought Walter had great talent. He used to write of bare-breasted young females treading their varying ways through life on moonbeams. It was simple, and it was sex. But that's long past. He's gone through four analysts and as many different periods. Each analyst seems to have made him a little more complex in his writing, until now not even the critics can understand him."

"Sometimes," I said, "that's the best way."

"You're rather philosophical for a"—she laughed—"a private eye, I think the term is."

Mabel returned with a tray with two glasses on it. She placed the tray on a small table before Mrs. Pendleton. The latter stooped over slightly, picking up one of the glasses; she held it beneath her nose for a fraction of a second, then passed it on to me.

"I hope you don't mind my sniffing at your drink, Mr. Phelan," she said. "It's been so long since I've had one for myself, that it's about the only enjoyment left me, to sniff at one."

I sipped at the "iced tea." It was about the best bourbon I'd ever tasted. I grinned at Mrs. Pendleton.

"And now that I've bribed you," she said, "you may tell me just how successful you've been in getting back those negatives."

I looked at Mabel. She was still wearing that permanent smile. I shrugged.

"Come, come, Mr. Phelan," Mrs. Pendleton said. "I've heard good things about you, even that you're intelligent. Don't play coy with me. I'm an old woman and for all practical purposes, dead. I just need a little dirt thrown over my face to make it official. I know that Walter hired you to get the negatives of those photographs of Honor."

"It's true I'm working for your husband, Mrs. Pendleton," I said. "But I make it a habit to never divulge any of my clients' business."

"Habits are nauseous."

"Regardless of that, what goes on between a client and myself is confidential."

I finished the glass of bourbon. I put the glass back on the tray. Mrs. Pendleton picked up the other one; she went through the sniffing routine before handing it to me.

"I've got a hollow leg, Mrs. Pendleton. I can sit here and drink these all day."

"The checkbook, please, Mabel," she said.

Mabel went over to a desk in one corner. She opened a drawer, then brought checkbook and a pen back to Mrs. Pendleton. I could see the old woman writing my name on the check. She dated it, then paused.

"The amount?" she asked. "You name it, Mr. Phelan."

I smiled, and said: "Let's pick out a round figure. Say, ten thousand."

"All right," she said. "That seems round enough."

She finished making out the check, then handed it to me. I took it and looked at it. The figure was for $10,000. I tore up the check. Sometimes, I think I'm pretty damned dumb; sometimes, there's little doubt about it.

Mabel chuckled softly in the background.

Mrs. Pendleton said: "I like strong men, Mr. Phelan. One meets so few of them. I could learn to like you."

I said, "You'd be lonely in the crowd, Mrs. Pendleton."

Mabel's chuckles increased.

Mrs. Pendleton sighed deeply. She stared out the window.

"It's a beautiful day," she said. "That's my son out there, Mr. Phelan. Joel."

I followed her stare. A tall slim figure was outside on the lawn, driving golf balls out of sight. A gigantic Russian wolfhound stood beside him, seemingly guarding him.

"That's quite a dog," I said.

"Most people say that," said Mrs. Pendleton. "They notice the dog, but not my son."

The tall slim figure moved away to disappear from my slight, the Russian wolfhound padding along beside him.

"I need your help, Mr. Phelan," Mrs. Pendleton said. "And so I'm going to tell you a story. I'll warn you beforehand that I'm relying on your pity, so be prepared. You know who I am. You know who my father was. Harry Baum." She sort of rolled the name over her lips. "Harry Baum," she repeated. "The man with the touch of a genius. The man who could do no wrong. He had it, but he never knew where it came from, and that bothered him until the day he died from a heart attack in a cheap whorehouse. Everything he touched turned to gold. They called him the King Midas of the movie world. By the time I was ten"—she shrugged, a small, helpless shrug—"I knew everything there was to know. By the time I was fifteen, I was an old woman. Harry Baum had little or no time for me, and my mother was a half-crazed idiot. She died when I was eleven, a broken, neurotic woman, still shopping for $1.98 bargains when she had millions to spend. It was too much for her."

"Tough," I said.

"Yes, and then he had me on his hands, and I turned out to be an ornament, a pretty little thing he carried around with him to show to the world that Harry Baum was, after all, human. He used me, my god, he used me. I went to bed with half the male stars of Hollywood, usually as the closing agreement in a business deal. By the time I was twenty"—her eyes drifted across my face and lost themselves somewhere in the past—"well, let's just say, I was ready to die. But, I've lived. Somehow, I have. I don't know how or why. Life hasn't meant much to me in a long time. Everyone came to this house, people from all over the world, maharajahs, shahs, kings, plain old millionaires, senators, even a president once; everyone came to meet Harry Baum and his beautiful Cinderella of a daughter."

"But you married J. Walter Pendleton," I said.

"Protective coloration," she said frankly. "I needed a harmless husband around, for the sake of appearances. I tried on so many slippers that, well, when I finally married Walter, nothing much mattered any more. Walter was a poor little man with his nose always in some book, reading and learning and reading some more, trying desperately to retain some of the knowledge he picked up from the books, but always failing. He was as opposite to Harry Baum as black is to white. We've been married twenty-nine years. That's a long time. We've got the three children, but Walter's never been a father to them, and I've never been a mother. Joel's the oldest, but he doesn't count any more. He moves around like a vegetable in his own quiet world. Landrith"—she hesitated—"Landrith is the only one with any backbone. She left us. And Honor. My poor sweet little Honor. You know, Mr. Phelan, there was a definite purpose in that name. I never had any honor, and I wanted her to have all of it. But she turned out to be a—" She stopped, looking down at her hands. "I want something for Honor, Mr. Phelan. I want to do something for her, before I die."

I rose to my feet. I walked to the window, looking out. It had been quite a story. Uh-huh.

I said, without turning: "You want to buy her back, that's what you want, Mrs. Pendleton. You want to buy her back to erase a lifetime of nothing." I turned, facing her. "I don't think it works that way."

"It's got to," she said.

"You wanted pity from me," I said, "so I would help you. You know, I don't feel pity for you. I feel contempt."

Mabel went around behind Mrs. Pendleton, and began stroking the other woman's hair with loving hands.

"You won't help me?"

The eyes were on my face, pleading, pleading.

"No," I said, "I won't. I have one client. I'm booked up."

I walked to the door, then paused.

"Maybe," I said. "Maybe, this'll work out. Who knows?"

Her voice was soft. "Thank you."

I walked out of the room. She had wanted pity; she had striven for it: and, damn it, regardless of what I had said, she had touched something deep within me. I smacked my fist against the wall.

She was only human. She had been running after something for so damned long that she had forgotten what it was.

She wasn't alone.

CHAPTER SIX

DARKENING CLOUDS were playing piggy-back across the afternoon sky as I drove back towards Hollywood. Thunder rumbled distantly in the east, and lightning flashed its answering challenge from the west. The battle was on. A few big drops fell on the windshield; there was a moment of indecision from the old man up in the sky, and then it started coming down in buckets.

The Chamber of Commerce would call it "unseasonal"; the eastern papers would play it up big and cute, and millions of dumb jerks who had never even seen Southern California would laugh up their collective sleeves; and the radio and tee-vee comics would have subject matter enough for another two months.

But it was nice to me. I liked it. It made me happy. I even rolled down the car window and stuck my hand out in it and let my hand get good and wet. And why not? I was running around in my own particular little vacuum. I knew from nothing. I was working for fifty bucks a day plus. One guy already had been killed: or had he? Where had I gotten the idea he had been murdered? Had Lundeberg said that, or had it been in the papers? Maybe it was my imagination. I knew from absolutely nothing. I had been real smart with the police and with the Pendletons and with everyone; everyone, that is, but myself. Lundeberg had said Sanchez had been shot with a .38; had he used the word "murdered"? I couldn't remember. There had been no mention of the gun having been found.

I laughed. At what?

The windshield wipers made a constant, almost pleasant hum, grinding back and forth, back and forth; the only drawback was that the hum matched up with the one in my head.

And so it went. The long drive. The rain. The aloneness. The cars passed me, and I passed them. It's not a pretty drive, not in the rain. But it was Sunday. The license plates read Iowa and Indiana and Oregon and Pennsylvania and Texas and, occasionally, even California. The cars were jammed; boys and girls, men and women, straining at the windows, getting a look.

I had read once that twelve million tourists visited the Los Angeles area every summer. I could believe it. But if I thought I could get the Pendletons out of my mind by thinking about such things, I was just fooling myself—a game that bores me if I play it more than thirty seconds. I found myself concentrating not only on my driving, but on the memory of that hard rock of a cop handing me a photograph across a messy desk, of that guy in the photograph—that young punk spread out on a heavily flowered carpet with a couple of holes from a .38 spoiling his shirt-front. And I mulled over the other photographs, the ones of a good-looking young kid with a good start in the world sinking low enough to pose for pornography, doing it of her own free will, enjoying it; and that was the rub, the enjoying of it.

That reminded me of something else to think about. Who had been the photographer?

What in hell, Phelan, what in hell? Why weren't you an accountant or a ditch digger or a truckdriver or a bank clerk or any goddamned thing but a private eye?

A good question. The only trouble with it was that it was unanswerable to the guy who had asked it. Me.

I let myself feel sorry for myself for one more minute, than I laughed and said the favorite four-letter word I reserve for just such occasions.

That was that. I felt better.

It was just a block off Sunset, on a street running north over the beginnings of a hill. Higher up, the rent probably ran two or three hundred per month; down here, about half that. Still a lot of money for a Mexican kid from the east side.

The place turned out to be a three-story stucco building with false red-iron balconies in front of each window and bougainvillea reluctantly climbing the wall. The building faced west, against the setting sun if there had been a setting sun, which there wasn't then; there was only the rain, and it was slanting against the building, making it an even uglier gray than it should have been.

I cramped the Dodge into a parking space, and sat there, finishing a pipe. I couldn't see any cops around, but then they probably wouldn't stake out where I could see them anyway. There was a room in that building which I wanted to get a look at. The question was whether or not the look was worth the risk. There could be a cop in the lobby; there could be one planted elsewhere in the building, even in the apartment itself. But I still wanted to get a look. I had an idea that they, meaning the police, wouldn't have been searching for the same thing that I would search for, providing I got inside that room.

Making up my mind, I stepped out of the car. I ducked through the rain and ran up the short steps into the lobby. It was small and unpretentious for that neighborhood: black and white marble walls, a pay phone with less than the usual number of obscene scribblings alongside it, and three even rows of brass mailboxes.

The only name that meant anything to me was in the slot box for 205: Memo Sanchez.

There was a self-service elevator, but I ignored it and walked up the stairs to the second floor. Not a soul in sight. Everything nice and quiet. The hallway was neat and clean, the carpeting looked fairly new and was in good taste, and the only objection I had to the place was the faint odor of cleaning fluid hanging in the air.

There were six apartments on the floor, three on each side; 205 was the last one on the north side. I walked by it, slowly, and down to the window at the end of the hallway. A fire escape ran down the side of the building, disappearing into an alley.

I walked back to 205. I put my ear to the door, but couldn't hear any movement on the other side. I took out my key ring and was debating which of the filed keys to try first when music drifted against my back; it wasn't loud and it wasn't bothersome.

"I wouldn't do that if I were you." Her voice was deep, almost masculine, but still nice. "There's a cop in there."

I turned around.

She was standing in the doorway of 206, and there was a lot of her to stand there. She was almost six feet tall, big-boned, but not heavy. She had hair that looked as if it might really be the color it was, a soft reddish-gold, worn in long, loose waves down to her shoulders. She was wearing a short terry-cloth robe that hit her high on her well-tanned, well-molded thighs, and I couldn't tell what else. She was barefoot, and she wriggled her toes against the thick carpeting. She wasn't wearing any makeup, just her natural face, which was all right with me. She had a pair of red harlequin eyeglasses in her right hand; she lifted them up to eye-level, peered at me for a moment, and then smiled.

I said: "That would be a horrible waste of talent."

"What would be?"

"If you were me."

The smile grew into a brief laugh. She brought the glasses up again, again gave me the once-over.

I heard the door to 205 opening behind me: I was causing quite a traffic jam in that hallway. I started to turn around, but she was quicker. She stepped out into the hallway; her arms curled around my neck, and she brought me in close. I certainly wasn't fighting it. Her mouth was strangely cool, and it moved in a lot of different directions and I wasn't thinking anything but one thing when someone cleared his throat behind me. She stepped back. The wink was ever so slight.

The guy cleared his throat again, and I turned around to look at him. He had plainclothesman written all over him. He was short and stubby, with that tired, worn look all cops get at a certain time in the day. He looked down at a fingernail, sighted something there, and hid the hand behind his back.

"I'm sorry to interrupt," he said. His eyes searched my face, and they went with the body: tired, worn.

"You should be," I said. "You come at a very delicate moment."

I could hear her suppressing deep laughter.

He opened his mouth to say something, but she beat him to the punch. "Oh, come on in, honey. Let's not stand around out here in the hall all day and give free shows."

I shrugged at him; you know, the what-the-hell-chance-have-I-got-shrug, and left him in the hallway all by his lonesome.

She closed the door behind her. She stood there for a moment, peering at me near-sightedly without the benefit of the glasses; she put them on and walked across the room.

It was a nice room to walk across; a soft red sofa, a matching chair, a couple of padded chairs that didn't match, a television set with a beach towel draped over its front, a stuffed bookcase, an unlit fireplace, walls full of Degas reproductions. A phonograph on a marble table in front of the sofa was playing softly.

It was Beethoven, I think, though it might have been Mozart. I'm never very sure.

She sat down on the sofa and crossed those thighs. She continued to look at me for a moment, then followed my gaze; she put her palms down on her thighs, hiding my view.

"It's raining outside," I said.

That went over big, as I had known it would.

"I could get in trouble over you," she said.

"You could?" I said eagerly.

"You might be the murderer."

"I might be, but I'm not." I hesitated. "You're not above suspicion."

She shook her head. "Isn't there something about murderers always returning to the scene of the crime?"

"There is," I said, "but that's only in fiction. Actually, it doesn't work out that way very often."

"The police seem to think it might, this time. That cop's been in there since last night."

"It figures."

"Yes," she said. She reached over, turning off the music. "You must have been anxious to get in there, I mean, you figured a cop might be in there but took the risk."

"I was anxious, maybe too anxious."

"Why?"

"Let's try another angle," I said. "How come you're playing the heroine and helping me out?"

She rose to her magnificent feet and walked across the room, disappearing through a doorway. She looked just as good from the rear as she did from the front, which is quite an accomplishment in this day and age. She came back, and this time she was wearing a pair of high-heeled shoes. She came up close to me. I still had a couple of inches on her. She smiled in a self-satisfied manner as she found out this fact.

She stepped back and kicked off the shoes. She, apparently, had something against footgear.

"Let's just say," she laughed, "that it's a Sunday afternoon and that it's raining outside and that the back of my head aches from too much television and that I've read every goddamned book in that bookcase and that they're a poor substitute for the real thing and that maybe I'm bored and that maybe I'm lonely." She dug beneath her hair and pulled at a pearly ear. "And let's also just say that you're the first man I've met in six months that's bigger than me, and I like it. I like the way your face is all beaten up. It suggests a lot of things. I may be a dope, but I like it."

"You're a beautiful dope, angel," I said. "I enjoyed that, out there. We'll have to do it again, real soon.

"Don't get all hot and bothered."

"I'm already that," I said. This girl could excite any man, and the last time I checked, that's what I was.

She laughed, and I noticed then, for the first time, that her eyes changed color when she did so. They were sort of greenish, but when she laughed, flecks of blue appeared from nowhere. It could be rather disconcerting.

"And now let's get back to you," she said.

I had nothing to lose.

I took out my wallet and gave it to her. She took it, opened it, studied the cards, then handed it back to me.

She walked away through another doorway into what I supposed was the kitchen. She still looked all right from the rear. I could hear the tinkling of ice cubes. She reappeared presently with a tall glass in each hand. She gave one of them to me. I sipped at it. Gin and tonic. Not bad.

She sat down on the sofa again, and this time she let me have my look: and I took it. She sipped from her drink, then put the glass down. She lit a cigarette, pushing the smoke towards the ceiling in one long jet. She adjusted the red harlequin glasses on her nose, took another sip from her drink, and then looked at me.

"Sit down, Mr. Phelan," she said, "or may I call you Johnny?" I sat down and nodded my head; I wouldn't have argued with her, whatever she wanted to call me. "Now that we're comfortable and the rain is patting down cozily on the roof, we can talk. I'll think up three subjects, and you take your choice. The effect of the Kinsey reports on the American sex life, the weather, or Memo Sanchez."

I said: "Sex is something for action, not talk. The weather stinks." I smiled what I hoped was my best smile. "That leaves the departed Mr. Sanchez."

"That's a helluva thing to be left with," she said.

"I suppose it is," I said. "But I have to earn a living, or what passes for one. Sanchez had something of importance to my present client. At least, I think he did. One is never sure about anything in this business. That's why I wanted to have a look at his apartment."

"The police already have gone over his apartment."

"I'm not a cop. Maybe my way of searching differs from theirs."

"Maybe." She looked the other way. "I'll bet I could guess what that something is."

"Why don't you try?"

"Photographs. Nice ones. The kind they sell down on Skid Row to pimply kids."

"You seem to know a lot about Sanchez."

She didn't say anything to that.

I looked out the french windows at one end of the room. The rain was maintaining a steady drumbeat against the panes. I could see brown-green hills in the distance, peeking through the dark clouds.

I said: "Did you mention the pictures to the police?"

"Do you take me for an idiot?"

"Of course not, angel."

"Will you please quit calling me that? My name is Jean Gibbon. And I didn't tell the police anything for a very special reason. I just didn't want to get involved. Is that so hard to understand?"

No. Not if it were true.

"Just how well did you know Sanchez?"

She measured the question before answering. "I had drinks with him on a few occasions, dinner once. Nothing more than that, though. He was a guy with quick ideas, but I never have liked men who think themselves irresistible to women. You know, he was a war hero and his brother was a fighter, that kind of thing. He made a lot of use of it. His idea of a big time was going straight to bed and then posing for pictures. He could be attractive to some women, I guess, and I can see where he'd get a lot of business."

"But none of yours?"

"None of mine," she said.

"I still don't get it," I said.

She studied a pale little ballerina on the wall.

"What do you do for a living, Jean?" I went on.

"You're worse than the cops. Much worse. Maybe I'm making a mistake about you."

"Maybe. It was just a question."

"Too personal to suit me. You kill me, Johnny."

"I'd like to do something more pleasant than that to you."

"I'll think about it," she said.

She drained her drink. She got up and came over to get my glass. I made a pass at her, but she ducked away. Her face had a curious seriousness about it that bothered me. I shrugged, and handed her my glass.

She went back into the kitchen. I got up, and followed.

She was standing by the sink, dropping fresh ice cubes into the glasses. Her shoulders were hunched forward beneath the robe. I put a hand on one of them, turning her to face me. She avoided my look for some time, and then I saw that there were tears crowding her eyes.

I chucked her under the chin in my best big-brother manner and she tried to smile, but it wasn't too successful.

"I'm a hard-boiled one, I am," she said.

"We all go soft, honey. It's part of the game."

She took a step backwards. She undid the robe and dropped it to the floor. She hadn't been wearing anything else. The thing that stood there facing me was just about the most gorgeous hunk of human flesh a man can dream of. Or a woman.

I felt the moistness in my palms and tried to look away, but it was a losing battle.

"Have a look, Johnny," she said. her voice small and tight. "It's for free. It won't cost you a penny, not one penny." The tears had become too much of a crowd; they were spilling around behind her glasses, and a couple slipped free, rolling down her cheeks. "Go ahead, Johnny. Have a look. Go on. Stare. That's what I'm for. Miss SeaVue of Astoria, Oregon. Miss SeaVue of 1953. That was the greatest thing that ever happened to me, Johnny. Sure, it was. They gave me a gold cup with my name on it, and my picture was in all the Portland papers. A great thing. And this guy from Portland, he owns a big department store there, and he's a funny guy, and he said he'd like to sponsor me. Get that word—*sponsor*. He said I had a great future in the movies. Sure, I did. He *sponsored* me, all right. He brought me down here and he kept me in a nice apartment for three long years and he'd come down once a month and we'd have a glorious weekend together and he'd do all the things to me he couldn't do to his fat old wife and a good time would be had by all."

"I bet I know what happened," I said.

"Yes … two years ago, he decided he'd had enough, or maybe it was his wife that decided for him. I don't know. And then I was stuck here. And then I met another guy, and then a couple more, and then Memo Sanchez. It was nice and easy. I just did the posing. It was an easy way to make money, good money, because I didn't have the guts to either go back to Astoria or try and get a decent job. I just didn't have the guts. So take a good look, Johnny. The merchandise is a little worn, a little used, but it's still good merchandise. It's yours, if you want it. Just say the word."

She finished. She took a deep breath, and looked down at the floor, then up at me again. She reached up, taking off the glasses, putting them down on the kitchen counter. She rubbed her eyes with the backs of her hands, and her teeth were working over-time on her lower lip.

Some dish, this. Some dish. Good ol' Phelan; he gets 'em all. He never misses a one.

"The only trouble, Johnny," she said, "is that I no longer like myself. It's a helluva situation. I'm ashamed of myself, of me, Jean Gibbon."

I stooped over and picked up the discarded robe. I put it around her shoulders, and tied the belt in front. My palms were still moist and I felt like a stud horse.

Only, I'm a chump. A first-class chump.

Big-hearted me.

She fell into my arms and had herself a good cry.

Hell, my shoulder was big, big enough for the whole world. I'm a whizz, I am.

CHAPTER SEVEN

THE AFTERNOON dragged by. No, that's not quite right: it went by pretty fast. The room grew dark, but we didn't bother with the lights. I built a fire in the fireplace, even though it wasn't cold enough for one. We spent the afternoon on opposite sides of the room. I lay on the sofa, enjoying the growing dark, enjoying the sounds of the crackling fire and the drumming rain, enjoying the knowledge that I could, at any time I wished, rise to my feet and possess that strange hunk of beauty across the room.

She had discovered a weak chink in my armor. It wasn't her body alone that had done it. There was something about her, a certain defenselessness, a certain way she had of convincing me that she was in above her head, a certain something that convinced me that, despite what she had done, it hadn't been her, the real her, who had done it.

Hell, a guy's got to relax once in a while, even a hard-boiled old monkey like myself.

She sat on the floor across the room from me, and talked; she stretched those long legs out in front of her, and rested her back against the seat of a chair, and she talked. I didn't pay much attention to what she said; I just listened to the sound of her voice.

Mr. J. Walter Pendleton wasn't getting much service for his fifty bucks a day plus. Not much at all.

The time wore on. The darkness became even darker, until the only light was a thin sliver of bouncing yellow upon the carpet, coming from the fireplace.

I heard her steps coming across the room. She was next to me then. And I felt her kisses on my lips. Kind of fumbling kisses, I thought, for one with her professed experience ...

I woke up, shattering the dream. Or had it been a dream? Sometimes it's hard to tell.

I lay there for a moment and let the pieces fall into place, and then I got up and searched around in the dark for some light. I did a lot of stumbling in the dark before I found any.

The room was the same as it had been, only the fire had gone out. What had I expected? I don't know.

I could hear water running, but it wasn't the rain; that had stopped long ago.

She was in the shower. It hadn't been a dream, after all. I walked through the bedroom and into the bathroom. She was humming, slightly off-key, a very romantic ballad, and I could just barely make out the outline of her body through the wrinkled-glass shower.

I said, "Hi," but she didn't answer; she didn't hear me.

I went back through the apartment, into the kitchen. I scrounged around, finally finding the coffee and the pot. I put them on the stove.

By that time, the noise from the shower had stopped. I trudged back in there. She was sitting in front of the dresser, a towel draped around her shoulders, brushing at that reddish-gold hair. She swung around to look at me. She pushed up her lips in a mock-kiss.

I grabbed hold of some of that hair; it was like silk, it was like—hell, I was acting like some teen-ager after his first big affair.

"Put some clothes on," I said. "You make me nervous."

She laughed. But she got up, slipping into a housecoat that didn't hide enough of her.

We sat at the kitchen table and drank the coffee.

I said, "I'm not doing much to earn my keep."

She started to laugh again, then apparently saw something on my face, and stopped. "What can you do, Johnny? It's something for the police to handle, not you. They get paid to find murderers."

"And I get paid to protect certain interests. I'm not doing that now."

"Johnny," she said, "I'll help you in any way I can. Honest, I will."

"Okay," I said, "begin."

"How?"

"We'll start with Saturday night, or evening. Were you home?"

"Part of the time, yes."

"Did you hear the shots?"

"No."

"Did you hear anything else?"

She hesitated; then: "No."

"Did you see anything?"

She shook her head.

"You're helping a lot, honey. A helluva lot."

"I'm sorry," she said.

"You sure you didn't hear anything?"

She shook her head again.

"What time were you home?"

"I went to a matinee, in Hollywood. I got back here sometime around six. I'm not sure of the time."

"And you're quite sure you neither heard nor saw anything unusual?"

"You keep asking me that. Why?"

"I want the truth."

She didn't answer.

"Did you stay in the rest of the evening?"

"Yes."

"What did you do?"

"Nothing. There wasn't anything to do."

She lit a cigarette. I noticed her hands were nervous, trembling a little.

"Johnny," she said. "I want to thank you. I mean, for being around this afternoon. Not for the"—she looked at me—"not for that, but for the other. I've had that crying jag coming on for a long time, too long a time. I'm glad it was you who was here to pick up the pieces."

Good ol' John J. Phelan.

"I'll level with, Johnny. I told you I posed for some photos. It was easy money, and I like things the easy way. But I never did mix in with Sanchez much. It was just a business arrangement. That, you've got to believe."

"You're a good one," I said. "Real good."

I filled a pipe, but I didn't light it.

She looked at the pipe in my hands. "I didn't know you smoked a pipe," she said.

"Now you do," I said. "Did you pose alone, or was there a guy in the pictures with you?"

She looked at me for a long, still moment. There was no sound in the kitchen, nothing.

And then she said, "So that's it. I didn't know."

"Stop it," I said. "You'll have me believing you."

"Johnny, I posed in the nude from the waist up. That's all, and if you don't believe me, you can go to hell."

"I've been there and back again."

"Johnny, what gives with you? I know I'm not much good. You come in here prancing around like some kind of royalty, and I fall all over myself. I saw you, and something flipped inside me. So help me, something flipped inside me. You want to laugh, go ahead. It's corny and nuts, and I don't deny it."

It was corny and nuts. I didn't deny it, either. I just looked at her.

She said: "All right, you want to know so bad, then I'll tell you. I heard the shot. It frightened me, but I went to the door and peeked out into the hallway there. Memo's door was slightly open, and I could hear someone—it sounded like a woman—giggling in his apartment. I closed my door and came back in here and sat down and did a lot of thinking and decide to hell with it, I wouldn't open my mouth. And I didn't, not to the police, at any rate."

"You heard just one shot?"

"That's right."

I tried to remember that photograph of Memo Sanchez; I was sure there had been two holes in him.

"What time was that?"

"I'm not exactly certain. Some time between six and six-fifteen. As I said, I'd been to a matinee."

"Why didn't you tell this to the police?"

"Johnny, I'm in enough trouble. I know Memo was in a racket, supplying those pictures to someone. I'd rather chance it out with the police than with some trigger-guy."

"But you said it was a woman giggling."

"I don't care what I said. I just don't want to get involved. I don't."

"Okay," I said.

I reached up, pulling her head down to mine. I kissed her. It would always be the same, whatever she had been; I didn't care.

She pulled away from me, and laughed a little laugh, and sat down again. "This is crazy," she said. "It doesn't add up."

"Does anything, ever? Look, Jean, did you see any of the boys Sanchez ran with?"

"No, no one but the photographer who took the pictures."

"What's his name?"

"That I don't know. A fat little man. Memo called him Neal, but that's all I know about him."

We kissed again. It was getting to be a habit.

I said, "How'd you like to go out tonight? Dinner, dancing, that kind of thing?"

She smiled. "I thought you'd be the type that didn't dance."

"I don't," I said, "but you can teach me."

"Give me five minutes."

"Sure. I'm sorry I was rough on you. I just like to know what's going on, that's all."

"Don't explain yourself to me, Johnny. I like you just the way you are."

She ran into the other room to get dressed. She was like a young kid happy over her first big date: and maybe I was, too. Who knows? Something like a conscience touched me, but that's all it did: I didn't let it run away with itself.

Hell, she was old enough to know what she was doing.

But was I?

She was ready in five minutes on the dot. She was a vision. She was wearing a reddish-polka-dot thing that went with her hair; there wasn't much above the nippleline.

She whirled around to give me a look-see and, despite my age and physical condition, she didn't know how close she came to not going out that night.

Maybe it would have been better that way.

CHAPTER EIGHT

The red barn stands just across the Ventura County line near that state highway running through the horse country on its way to Ventura and, farther up, Santa Barbara. It's the part of Southern California most of the movie studios use for their westerns: rugged, rolling hills, red in the daytime, with huge boulders looming here and there across the scene almost as if some director had ordered it that way; from behind them the dirty redskins can jump a wagon train or a line of cavalry at any moment.

The side road led off the main highway around a slight curve, and dipped into a cup set between high boulders. The barn itself was a high, two-story affair that looked as if it might actually have been a barn at one time. Below it, stretching out to the west, lay the beginnings of Sima Valley. Lights blinked crazily from the tiny town of Dorsett right at the foot of the butte.

There was plenty of parking space, but still it seemed unusually crowded for a Sunday night. I guess most people aren't particular about what night they lose their money, as long as they lose it and get a good run for it. There were no neon lights, no signs of any kind. Richie Egan didn't need to advertise: his kind of business never does.

A husky youngster in levis took the Dodge from us, and Jean and I crunched up the gravel walk to the entrance. A big, tough-looking monkey stood at the door, his barrel-like arms crossed over his chest; he was wearing a tuxedo and a bored expression, but the boredom flickered away as he glanced at Jean.

He finally tore his eyes from her and gave me a swift inspection.

I said, "Think the rain'll hurt the rhubarb?"

He snarled but let us pass.

The lobby was spacious and expensive. A poster took up one wall. The girl in the poster was leaning against a piano, one arm outstretched, her mouth opened in song, looking quite beautiful in the spotlight. The name below, in bix letters, said Lannie Dixon. I had met her as Landrith Pendleton.

The hostess was tall and willowy and carried a bunch of gigantic menus in one hand. She gave Jean that look women reserve for women that look like Jean, and then gave me a big smile. She must have thought I was really something to be carting around a showpiece like Jean. I told her we would have dinner first.

She led us past a short bar. A few stallions were lolling about on the stools, looking over the field. They spotted Jean, and rolled about on the stools, crossing and recrossing their legs as we walked by. I would never be noticed that night, not at least by a normal male with normal instincts: or maybe they're subnormal or supernormal; I don't know.

Egan was a smart cookie, of that, I was sure. His waitresses were all tall and willowy, like the hostess, and all big-busted. They all wore white gingham shorts and red tops that left a lot showing and mesh stockings that disappeared into the unknown. The one that took our order for two dry martinis and two medium-well filet mignons had a helluva time writing it all down; I was surprised that she could even write. But then, I guess that's the way Egan wanted it.

I had had one sip of that martini and was trying to look at something besides the gorgeous hunk of flesh opposite me, and failing, when another tough-looking monkey who could have been the doorman's twin, patted me on the shoulder, almost dislocating it.

The words came out low and slow, but I got the idea. I excused myself from Jean, and followed him out of the dining room. We walked down a hallway with numbered doors on either side of it and a lot of caricatures of movie people lining the walls and ended up in front of a door marked PRIVATE. The big guy rapped lightly, then opened the door, and beckoned for me to enter.

Landrith Pendleton was sitting on the edge of a desk in a long black thing that did as much for her as was possible; she was smoking a cigarette and looking quite peeved. There was a guy behind the desk, also smoking a cigarette. He stood up as I entered. He was about six-four, tending a little to stoutness around the middle, but still in good condition; his hair had just enough gray mixed in with the mass of curls to make a certain type and age of woman ooh-and-aah; he was pushing forty-five, but not too fast. He started to stick out a hand the size of the proverbial ham in my direction, then thought better of it, and looked at the other guy in the room. This one was curled up in a deep leather chair beneath a bunch of photographs of famous race horses. The expression on his face just about matched with the expressions of the horses. He had a thin piece of white tape beneath his right eye, and his own arms lay still on the arms of the chair.

I had seen him before. His name was Luis "Lulu" Sanchez.

Landrith Pendleton turned to look at me; there wasn't much in the look, just a hint of recognition.

I said, "You're interrupting my dinner."

The guy behind the desk nodded his mass of curls briefly. The door closed behind me; the big, tough-looking monkey had gone off to his cage again.

Now the matinee-type behind the desk said: "I'm Egan. Richie Egan. This is my place."

I said: "I'll now turn four handsprings and look to the heavans for guidance."

Egan said: "You're sharp with the words, friend. I'd heard that about you. Sharp and nasty. I don't like sharp and nasty guys. They annoy me."

"That's too damned bad," I said.

Landrith Pendleton laughed, seemingly against her own wishes, and said: "You two hit it off real well."

"He's cute," I said.

Egan breathed deeply, and sat down again. He crushed out his cigarette in an ashtray gigantic enough for half the world's old, tired butts, and I felt sure he was using that cigarette as a symbol for my head.

Sanchez picked at the piece of tape beneath his eye. He sighed in a bored manner, and said: "We got things to talk about, *amigo*."

"Run along, junior," I said, "and look for another setup."

His eyes narrowed. "You had an appointment with my brother. You showed up. He didn't. How about that?"

"Maybe you'd like to collect the ten grand?"

He got to his feet, slowly. He held his hands out in front of him, and looked at them. He was thinking about it.

I said, "Go ahead, junior, and try it. I got forty pounds on you, and I'm getting damned tired of being kicked around. A couple of guys called on me last night. They enjoyed what they did to me. I got an idea they were friends of yours, and I owe them something in return. If you want to collect it, come ahead."

Landrith Pendleton laughed, but it wasn't much. Sanchez threw dirty eyes at her, then sat down again.

"You got your hackles up, Phelan," said Egan.

"Yeah," I said.

"What do you want here?"

"Right now," I said, "I'm having dinner with a luscious redhead. Later on, I might go upstairs with the other suckers and risk a few hard-earned shekels."

"It's a losing proposition," said Egan.

"Depends what the proposition is," I said.

He thought about that. "You're sticking your nose in the wrong notches, shamus," he said. "Lay off or you're liable to get the nose cut off for you."

I felt my nose. "It's too big anyway."

He placed two huge hands palms down on the top of the desk, and leaned forward; he worked his mouth around for a minute, but didn't say anything, and then he looked at Landrith Pendleton. She was still looking at me, and it still didn't mean much. I got the idea she was calling the signals.

She said: "You're looking better than the last time I saw you. A little better, not much."

"Thanks, sweetheart," I said. "I feel fine." I looked at Egan. "How's the dirty picture business these days?"

That caught him, and hung him there for a minute.

Sanchez inhaled a lot of air, and looked at the ceiling.

Landrith Pendleton studied her hands.

"You're pushing your luck with me, Phelan," Egan said.

"A habit I have," I said.

Landrith Pendleton moved away from the edge of the desk. She took a couple of steps towards me, then stopped and shrugged. "You're a funny guy, Phelan. A real funny guy. We know what you're looking for; we know who hired you to look. We're looking for the same thing. Maybe our reasons are different, but I don't see why we can't pool our resources and save each other a lot of trouble."

"You don't, huh? I'm getting to be popular. I don't know why. Everyone wants to hire me, and I'm the kind that works for one client at a time."

"You could change," she said.

"I'm too old for that."

Egan growled something unintelligible.

"What time do you feed him his raw meat?" I asked.

Her face showed disappointment. She shook her head; she lifted one hand, then dropped it uselessly to her side. Egan came around from behind the desk. He reached me in two long strides and slapped me across the mouth with an open palm. It stung, and I tasted blood. I smiled it away and looked at him, and then he laughed; it was a big laugh, fitting his build.

"I like you, Phelan," he said.

He stuck his right hand out and I stepped inside it and hit him right in that beginning stoutness around the middle. He grunted harshly and stooped over; he fought for his breath for a while, then straightened upright again.

His smile was a lot like my own.

"I don't like guys slapping me in the mouth," I said. "Not even big guys like you, Egan. And, from what I hear, Mr. Egan, you are really big. I hear you run the books on the west side. That, together with your take here, makes you big, Mr. Egan. But just don't step on me." I hesitated. I studied the horses on the wall, and listened to that little thing beating inside my chest; it was the only sound in the room. I chanced a shot in the dark: "Memo Sanchez was a damned big bettor. Too big for his own britches. I heard, just this morning, that he had a few outstanding tabs against his name. That'd be bad for your business, wouldn't it, Mr. Egan?"

Egan's eyes narrowed. He was appreciating me more and more. A funny look passed over Sanchez's face; he stared at Egan, started to say something, and then changed his mind.

"You're brighter than I thought, Phelan," said Egan. He added: "I could have you torn apart. I've got goons working for me that enjoy that kind of thing."

"You could," I said, "but you won't. It wouldn't do you any good."

"I suppose not," he said.

He stuck his right hand out again, and this time I took it. We gave each other a few love-squeezes, and then we both decided to call it a draw. He laughed again.

"I shouldn've known better, Phelan," Egan said. "Lannie is always right. She had you pegged, but I wouldn't believe her. I had to be shown. You're okay, Phelan. You'll do."

"Thanks," I said, "but no thanks."

I looked at her. She looked at Egan.

Sanchez cleared his throat. "*Did* Memo owe you money, Egan?"

Egan swirled around to look at him. "Don't jump on the wrong horse, Lulu."

I said: "What's your pitch in this, Egan?"

He looked at me again, and said: "No reason why we shouldn't play ball together, Phelan. We're all in the same game, so we might as well keep it in the family. Lannie's old man wants those photos; she wants them, too, and she doesn't want him to get them, and what she wants I help her get."

"Why?"

He shook his head, ignoring me. "I got an idea that who-ever's got the negatives also rubbed out Memo. That's where Lulu comes in. These Mexicans have got strong family ties; he doesn't like the idea of his brother being rubbed."

"It's all nice and sweet," I said.

"No reason why we shouldn't play together, is there?"

"One reason," I said.

"And what would that be?"

"You're lying to me, Egan," I said.

His facial muscles rippled smoothly.

"You do take chances, friend," he said.

"I get paid for it," I said.

"It's your neck," he said.

"I thought it was my nose."

He didn't say anything; he just stood there, and twiddled his thumbs. We let the silence thicken a bit. Egan walked around behind the desk and sat down and twiddled his thumbs some more. Sanchez was watching him, still with that funny look on his face. There were a lot of undercurrents here.

I chanced it: "Lulu, here, has got the prints, Egan. I still don't know where the negatives are."

"You're a goddamned liar, Phelan," the fighter said.

Egan nodded his head. He stopped the twiddling and made a temple with his hands, looking at Sanchez.

"What do you take me for, Richie?" asked Sanchez. "You think I'm nuts. I got a …"

"Take it easy, Lulu," said Egan. His voice was clipped and low.

I let them have some more: "I told you a couple of goons called on me last night. They were sweet kids. They beat the holy be-jesus out of me and got the prints Pendleton had left with me. I could be wrong about this, but I doubt it. I think those guys were working for Lulu."

"He's screwy, Richie," said Sanchez.

"Ask her." I pointed at Landrith Pendleton.

"Some of it's right, Richie," she said. "Someone did beat the hell out of him. I got there right after it happened."

"I don't know nothing about it," said Sanchez.

"One of these birds was a fat little Mex," I said. "The other one had a wrinkled scar under his left eye. If you ever find them, hold them for me. I owe them a few kicks."

Sanchez's expression was pained.

"We'll see about it," said Egan.

I was doing my bit.

"Goddamn," said the Mexican. He looked at me. "I got ideas about you, too, you sonofabitch."

"How dumb are you, Egan? You think Memo was in on the picture business by himself? This monkey watched me more at that fight last night than he did Kid Frisco."

"I ain't taking that from you."

The kid bounded across towards me. I met him with a well-placed shoe right in the groin. He grunted, and sat down on the floor, holding his hands over his groin. Neither Landrith nor Egan offered to help him.

I said: "My filet's getting cold, and I got an investment to protect out there. I'll just toddle along like a good little boy."

"Order another filet," said Egan, watching Sanchez sitting on the floor. "It's on the house."

"That might be," I said, "but the redhead isn't."

I walked to the door, then stopped there. There would be a lot of conversation going on after I left. I would have enjoyed hearing some of it.

"I like to do things my own way, Egan," I said. "Another bad habit."

"You're full of bad habits," said Landrith Pendleton.

"If you need any help," said Egan, "call on me."

"Sure," I said. "I'll do that."

Landrith Pendleton's voice was almost a whisper. "Your kind of guy never needs any help, Phelan. Never. You always know best. You think."

"I love you, too, sweetheart," I said.

"I'll think about that in my dreams," she said.

I closed the door after me.

CHAPTER NINE

Jean wasn't at the table when I got back. I didn't think much about it; not then. After all, nature calls, even a beautiful one like that. The stallions were still lined up at the bar; there was a certain smugness about them as they looked at me, but I ignored that.

I ordered two fresh martinis and then Landrith Pendleton came on to do a couple of numbers. She stood in the shimmering spotlight and moved around the scant dance floor. Her voice wasn't much, but it didn't have to be. She had all the proper sensuous body movements, and no one was listening to her voice anyway; no one, that is, but me. I had nothing else to do.

Her first number was a love ballad with too many double meanings in it; her second number was sung straight, and right at me. She was working too hard.

Polite applause greeted her finish. She came over to my table. She sat down without being invited.

"You threw a lot of dirt around in there," she said. "You think you're pretty smart. You got them growling at each other like a couple of dogs."

"That's too bad," I said, not looking at her.

A five-piece combo came on to furnish some dance music for those who didn't want to lose their money upstairs or for those who already had.

"I feel like an old used dishrag," she said.

"What?"

"You're looking at everything here but me."

I shrugged.

"II can't blame you much," she said. "I got an eyeful of that one when you came in. That's a lot of woman."

I looked at her, and smiled. I don't know why, but I did. "Keep your chin up, sweetheart. There's enough to go around."

Nature was a long time in being answered. I signaled for the waitress, a funny little feeling forming in the middle of my stomach. I asked her if she had seen the girl who had been with me. "Why, yes," she said, "she left some time ago."

"Alone?"

"No. With a man. I thought ... "

But I didn't listen to any more.

I sat there, and let it sink in. That funny little feeling grew some and I felt like putting my head under a meat-cleaver. I looked at Landrith Pendleton. She appeared puzzled.

"So help me—" But I didn't get any further than that. That big, tough-looking monkey was out of his cage again. I was again wanted in the office. I said, no thanks, not this time, but the gun he held in the palm of his right hand convinced me otherwise.

Landrith Pendleton followed us.

It was crowded in the office. Sanchez was back in the deep leather chair, a self-satisfied grin marring his face, and Egan was still looking pretty behind his desk. Another big, tough-looking monkey stood against one wall, a dumb look on his sour face. A short, stocky guy with close-cropped gray hair wearing a leather jacket and a .45 strapped around his middle was standing next to a chair in which a frail little thing with a mass of peroxided hair was hiding; she had her face stuck in a handkerchief, and her shoulders were heaving.

I felt something, but I didn't know what it was.

The short, stocky guy turned to look at me. His lips flattened over his yellow teeth, and he touched the girl on the shoulder. She looked up at me with tear-stained eyes and said, "That's him;

that's the one," and then went back to her handkerchief and her sobbing.

"Okay, wiseguy," the short, stocky one said.

I looked at Egan. He shrugged playfully.

The short, stocky guy grabbed me roughly, enjoying it. He smelled like he had been bathing in his own sweat for at least a month. He reached in the pocket of his leather jacket. He had the cuffs around my wrists before I even knew what had happened.

The girl in the chair looked up at me again. "You … you … " she started, but didn't finish.

"Okay," I said, "what is it?"

"You know damned well what it is, wiseguy," the short, stocky guy said. He jabbed me in the ribs. "We don't like your kind out here."

Sanchez laughed loudly, and shook his head.

Egan said: "This young girl says you molested her, Phelan. She says you pinched her in the wrong places and made indecent proposals. I'm surprised at you."

Holy Christ!

Egan went on: "This is Chief of Police Hunter of the Dorsett police force." The smile was very slight. "As a matter of fact, he's the whole police force."

Sanchez continued to laugh loudly.

I was in it up to my crotch, and maybe more. Dorsett was probably owned by Egan, or he could buy it; it didn't make much difference. He wanted me out of the way, and he was getting his wish.

Hunter grabbed me roughly and started pushing me towards the door. I jerked away from him, and turned back to Egan.

"Egan," I said, "so help me Christ, if you harm one hair of that girl's head, I'll kill you with my own two hands."

Hunter jabbed me again.

The smile went away from Egan's face. He was either a damned good actor, or he didn't know what I was talking about.

I was going to have a lot of time to think about it.

CHAPTER TEN

THE DORSETT JAIL was one of those quaint little places. It had thick adobe walls and had probably been built sometime around 1800 by a Spanish wanderer who had gotten this far before finding a brown-cheeked Indian girl to his liking. It had one cell containing an old army cot, an equally old army blanket, and two playful mice; there was enough space left over to make a small office in which sat an old-fashioned rolltop desk, two swivel chairs, and—I would imagine when he had nothing better to do, which probably wasn't too often—Chief of Police Hunter.

He hadn't been very gentle with me. He didn't like "city wise-guys"—which was what he seemed to think I was—coming out to his little hamlet and pinching the local girls on their behinds. If I had been fool enough to have pinched this one, it wouldn't have been on her behind: it would have been right between the eyes and there would have been a few knuckles along with the pinch.

But I guess I couldn't blame her. It was my own fault.

Hunter had shoved me into the cell, not bothering to remove the handcuffs: they were a joy to wear. I looked around, and asked him where the toilet was. He showed me a good deal more of his yellow teeth, and pointed to the corner. I could smell what he meant.

But later, after he had serenaded me for a couple of hours by strumming on an antiquated guitar, he relented enough to bring around an old chipped enamel chamber pot.

He probably thought he was doing me a big favor.

I spent a great night.

The two mice played hide-and-seek all night long; the army cot had a long tear in it in which I had to put either my head or my rear end; and the blanket still had most of the cooties left over from World War I.

The morning wasn't much better.

I don't know which was worse, my hunger or my nausea. I had never gotten to that filet, but every time I started thinking about food, that urine smell from the corner would intervene, and the nausea would come on.

A great life. Yeah.

I hadn't thought about Jean Gibbon. I couldn't think about her, not and keep my sanity. This was a game in which the chips were human lives. I would have batted my head against the wall if I had thought too much about her.

Adam Wheeler stood with his hands in his pockets, an unlit cigarette stuck in one corner of his mouth. His features had a curious, lined expression about them, and then I saw that the lines were being caused by the age-old bars of the cell.

He smiled, and said: "You can get into more trouble than anyone else I know, even my own kids."

I didn't say anything. Sleep had managed to catch up with me for a few short minutes, but I certainly didn't feel in the least rested.

He smiled again, and said: "You've been a bad boy, Johnny. You should know better than to pinch little girls."

"Go to hell," I said. "It's not that funny."

The smile changed shape.

"I can leave you here," he said.

I looked out into the office. Hunter wasn't around.

"Where's the honorable Chief of Police?"

"Down at the corner filling station making a phone call. He doesn't do a thing without orders from Egan."

"How'd you know I was here?"

"We were watching the Gibbon girl. You were tailed out to Egan's last night."

He struck a match against the wall and lit the cigarette. He handed it to me through the bars. I inhaled deeply. The tobacco didn't mix well with my empty stomach.

"I guess I'm slipping in my old age," I said.

"You were too busy watching that redhead," he said. "I don't blame you. I'm a married man."

"Tough."

"Uh-huh."

"That song-and-dance you gave Johnson yesterday didn't work either, Johnny. He had you spotted. You should've known better. Now you've got Lundeberg all upset, wanting to know the connection between you and the Gibbon girl."

"You'd never believe me, Adam."

"Try me."

I looked at him. How many times over how many years had I done that?

Maybe it was the morning, maybe it was the jail, maybe it was something else, but something Wheeler had said finally registered with me.

"You said you were watching the Gibbon girl?"

He nodded.

"Where did she go last night?"

He shrugged. "That, we don't know. We had a man on your tail; he followed you out to The Red Barn, saw you go back to Egan's office, so he decided to slip in the can for a minute. When he came back out, the girl was gone."

"Oh, for Chrissakes, Adam!"

He gave me a funny look and backed away from the bars.

My hands were gripping the bars, trying to rip them out.

"Take it easy, Johnny," he said.

Sure, take it easy. I swung around. I picked up the chamber pot and smashed it against the wall; I smashed it again and again. I picked up the army cot and broke it into a hundred little pieces.

It was then that Hunter came back. He jumped across that jail surprisingly fast for one his size and build; he held a .45 right on me and said, "Cut that out, Phelan. That's city property you're tearing up."

I turned around and looked at him. "You can go straight to hell, Hunter, the quickest way, you and that sonofabitch you work for, Egan. I told him, and now I'm telling you. If something's happened to that girl, I'll rip you apart, cop or no cop."

He balanced the .45 easily in his right hand. He didn't scare much. If Wheeler hadn't been there, I would have been a dead man: it showed in his eyes. His finger slipped around the trigger guard, but he didn't have the guts, not in front of a witness.

He smiled that dull little smile of his with all the yellow teeth, and stuck the .45 back in its holster. He looked from Wheeler to me and then back to Wheeler. He slipped out a key and unlocked the cell door. I walked out into the room. He took out another key and removed the handcuffs. I rubbed my wrists and let everything die down within me. He stood there with that smile in front of those yellow teeth, just wanting me to try something; he really wanted it: it would have given him an excuse.

But I wasn't ready. Not then. I'd already been too dumb.

"You owe me fifty bucks for destroying city property," he said.

"I'll mail you a check," I said.

"You'd better do that," he said. "If you're ever in Dorsett again, Mr. Wiseguy, it won't be so simple for you. I've got ways of handling punks like you."

"Go choke," I said.

I left him doing that, and went outside.

I breathed deeply, calming down. A few Mexican farm workers were drifting along the street, and it wasn't much of a street: there was a filling station on the corner, a combination drygoods and drug store, a bar, and the jail. Not much. I wondered how many of those Mexicans this Hunter had beaten up; he would be the kind of a guy to do things like that.

Wheeler came out and stood beside me.

"I've never seen you blow up like that before, Johnny."

"I had it coming."

He nodded. "I'll drive you up to your car."

We got into his car, but he turned the wrong way, west, and started in that direction. I looked at him.

"There's a diner out here," he said. "We'll have some breakfast."

I didn't care what I did.

Breakfast wasn't much. Old toast. Old eggs. Old coffee.

I still didn't care.

Over the second cup of old coffee, Wheeler said: "What's got into you, Johnny? You're acting crazy."

I said: "Adam, you're an honest cop. I'd say that nine out of ten cops I've ever met have been honest. It's a dirty and a stinking job, and no one appreciates it, the taxpayers least of all. But that fat sonofabitch is no more a guardian of the law than any two-bit hunkie up in San Quentin. He's cheap and he's no good and he pains me."

"That's not what's bothering you."

"No," I said, "it isn't."

We looked at each other through the clouds of cigarette smoke. Good old Adam.

"She really got to you, didn't she?"

"I guess so," I said. "But it's not only that. I figured her for a lead in this thing. I took her to The Red Barn for a purpose last night. If anything's happened to her ..." I left it unfinished; there didn't seem to be any way to finish it.

"You could have squared with us the other night, downtown," he said. "Maybe we could have prevented some of this."

"Maybe," I said. "Hindsight."

"Who's your client, Johnny. What're you after?"

"You know better than that."

He shrugged, and said: "I can draw the picture. We know Sanchez wasn't a clean guy. The vice squad had been tapping him for some time. He was supplying photos down on Skid Row. That, and a couple of other things. Most of his models were either frustrated wives out for a thrill or hard-up young girls seeking a quick buck. We don't figure he was killed because of business competition. We figure he got hold of something big, and tried to cash in on it." He shook his head. "Maybe blackmail, something in that line. The people we have a line on don't have that kind of money."

I just sat there, so he went on. "We had a hunch about the Gibbon girl. We thought she knew more than she had told us. We know she worked for him. You must know something about her, Johnny, that we don't."

"Adam," I said, "this is a screwed-up business."

"Sure," he said. "Why don't we pool our money together and buy a farm some place. That's the life."

"Uh-huh," I said. "We'd go nuts in a week. How're the kids?"

"Oh, they're getting along. Little Adam's getting to be a problem, a goddamned problem. He's got to the point where he's interested in baseball and girls. He spends his mornings over next door in the neighbor's garage playing doctor, and his afternoon's playing ball. He can't seem to make up his mind which is the more important."

I couldn't tell him. Not me.

Wheeler took out two more cigaretttes. I held the match for them.

He said: "The Gibbon girl's background isn't so clean, Johnny."

"I know about her."

"You do, huh? All of it?"

"All I want to know."

"It's like that?"

I let him draw his own conclusions.

I watched the waitress. She was a big-breasted, round-faced Mexican kid with pipestem legs. She walked across to put a coin in the gaudy nickelodeon in one corner of the diner. The music was too loud. The waitress began dancing with herself in one corner. A fat old woman with hard lines around the corners of her mouth came out from the kitchen. She loooked at Wheeler and me, and then at the girl. The girl stopped her dancing. She swung up on a counter stool and began reading a movie magazine.

Dreams. Dream a little more. It was all she could do.

I began: "A client came to me Saturday. A daughter of his had had some dirty pictures taken of herself. In one of them, there was this guy, Sanchez. My client wanted me to get the negatives. He was worried about his wife, what effect the photos would have on her if she ever saw them. Right after my client left, a guy called me and offered me the negatives for ten grand. He told me to meet him at the fights that night." I stopped, and looked up at the ceiling. Dead flies lay in a gummy substance. "You know the rest of it, Adam."

"Do I?"

"All you need to know."

And that seemed true. There were some things I'd left out: but they had to be left out.

"Sanchez was the guy that called you?"

"I don't know that. His voice was muffled over the phone. Besides that, I'd never talked to him before."

"I'll have to report this to Lundeberg."

I shrugged. "It won't make any difference."

"Sanchez was a guy with enemies," he said.

"Aren't we all?"

His smile was slight and a long time in coming.

I said: "How does his brother fit in?"

"That, we don't know, Johnny. He might bring in potential customers for the picture business. There are a lot of frustrated babes hanging around the gyms. We figure it that way, although the kid has kept his nose clean before this."

"And Egan?"

"Egan owns Lulu. There's a front for him, but Egan's money is behind it."

"Any chance of Egan being tied in with the picture business?"

Wheeler shook his head. "I don't think so, Johnny. It doesn't fit him. Egan's a smart cookie. We've got a folder full of stuff on him downtown, but he's never even been booked. He's smart, damned smart, almost too smart. He came out here from the east, twenty, twenty-five years ago, something like that. He got himself a few bit parts in the movies, and then suddenly got big-money backing. He's been operating high ever since. He's smooth and, so far, has been untouchable. He's had The Red Barn out here for about ten years, but this county doesn't seem to mind. We think he's running the books on the west side, but it's another thing to prove it. No"—he shook his head again—"it doesn't figure that Egan would get mixed up in anything like this. He's pretty smart, sticks close to the gaming side of the ledger."

Something he had said bothered me. I thought about it.

"He was in the movies?"

"Nothing big. Just a spear-carrier, the way I hear it."

"What studio?"

He shrugged. "I don't remember. Why, is it important?"

"It might be, Adam. It might be." The back of my head ached; I closed my eyes, then opened them again: nothing had changed. "How many times was Sanchez shot?"

Wheeler's long face grew thoughtful. He didn't answer my question for a long moment, then: "Twice."

"Uh-huh," I said. "What time?"

He pounded out a little tune against the side of his coffee cup with his spoon. "The coroner fixes the death time at approximately three-thirty, give or take a little. You know how those things are."

"Anyone hear the shots?"

"No. It just so happens no one was home at that time. We checked every apartment in the building."

"Who found the body?"

"What is this, Johnny? You know something we don't?"

"I don't know a thing, Adam. Not yet."

He continued with his music-making. "The guy in 203. He came over to borrow some ginger ale, he says. He's clean. We checked him all the way through. He doesn't figure in it."

Something wasn't kosher here; not by a long shot. Jean had heard a single shot some time between six and six-fifteen. An experienced coroner didn't make that kind of a mistake.

We sat there and stewed in our own thoughts for a while, then paid the tab and went outside. The waitress was still working on her dreams; it was senseless labor. The sun outside was beginning its baking for that day. It sapped me.

"I've got to find that girl, Adam," I said.

"I'll do what I can," he said.

We walked down to the filling station, and he went into the phone booth there. I stood around outside and tried not to think of anything; it was quite easy.

He came out of the phone booth. His face told me the story. He hunched up and scratched one ear and stared straight into the sun. "You don't have to find her, Johnny. She's been found. She floated in with the tide this morning, out at Malibu."

CHAPTER ELEVEN

I STEPPED INSIDE, closing the door behind me.

Why I had come back, I didn't know; but I was there, at any rate. Wheeler had gone out to Malibu to check the body. But first he had okayed my entering Jean Gibbon's apartment.

It hadn't changed, not outwardly at least. There were still the same Degas reproductions on the same walls, the same television set with the same beach towel draped over its front, the same stuffed bookcase, the same furnishings: everything was the same, only she would never see them again.

I sat down on the sofa and lit a cigarette and looked at all the pale little ballerinas on the walls; sweet, simple, untouched by all the bother and trouble of actually being alive. Maybe it was better that way.

Why had she been killed? Why?

Someone must have feared her; someone must have known that she had heard the shot at the later time. But she had told me she hadn't revealed that information to anyone, and I believed her. Could there be another reason? There had to be.

I sat there and finished the cigarette and then got up and went into the kitchen. The coffee pot was still on the stove; the two cups were still on the table. I picked up one of the cups. Coffee grounds made a dirty brown smudge in the bottom of it: a dirty brown smudge, a dirty brown smudge, a dirty brown smudge; it kept repeating itself over and over in my mind.

I took the cups over to the sink and rinsed them out beneath the faucet.

I opened the refrigerator door and looked inside: two cans of Budweiser, a Coke, a bottle of Schwepps quinine water, a quart of skim milk, three tomatoes wrinkled with age, a hunk of Swiss cheese growing dark around the edges, some scattered lettuce. Not much.

I took out one of the cans of Budweiser and searched around for an opener, finally finding one. The beer was nice and cold. But Jean hadn't been the type for beer. Or had she? What did I really know about her?

I left the unfinished beer on the counter and went back into the living room and again sat down on the sofa and again lit a cigarette and again looked at the pale little ballerinas: we were becoming fast friends.

I looked at that bookcase for a long time. I wanted to get up and go over and take a closer look, but I was afraid; there would be too much hidden there, too much about her personality.

I noticed then, for the first time, an envelope on the coffee table. I remembered it had been there the previous day. I picked it up and looked at it. The return address was scribbled in a loose, feminine hand, and had been smeared with a blotter: 209 Cedar Street, Astoria, Oregon.

I couldn't help myself. I opened it, and read:

Dear Daughter,

So nice to get your letter of the 11th. Dad don't understand why you can't come up here and see us for a week at least this summer. He is feeling much better than the last time you saw him. He don't drink quite so much now, just on Saturday nights. He loves you, daughter, and he misses you just as I do. We been saving our money and we just might be able to come down there to Hollywood this fall around Thanksgiving time and see you if you can't get up here this summer. It all depends on what your Uncle Lou does. Dad's trying to get him to mind the store for us but you know your Uncle Lou, he don't like doing favors for nothing. I'm not saying nothing against him because he is your uncle but you know how he is, so tight and all and of course dad can't afford to pay him anything for doing this. We'll just have to wait and see how it turns out I guess. Well daughter, no news really. Everything remains the same with us. Nothing ever changes around here. We miss you and love you, both of us, and we hope you are getting along well down there. I been reading some of those magazines that expose things as they really are down there and Hollywood seems to be a fast place. I do hope you are being a good little girl but I don't have to worry about my Jean, do I? Ha, ha. Oh, yes, before I forget it, thank you so much for the very pretty scarf you sent for my birthday. I wore it just last Sunday to the church picnic and it drew raves from one and all. I baked a tuna casserole for the picnic and it went over big. Joe Morrison was there and asked about you. I think he still cares but you know how men are with their pride and all. He's going around with Sue Jacobs these days. Well, I guess that is all. Again love from us both and thanks again for the scarf. Take care of yourself, daughter.

Love, Mother

Joe Morrison was there and asked about you … but you know how men are …

Sure, she had known how men were.

And how were they?

Joe Morrison. A good name. I could picture him; bigshouldered, bright-eyed, fretting over car payments, the way his boss looked down on him, wondering when and if and how it would happen. But what kind of a lunk was he, really? Why had he let her leave Astoria? She should have been at that church picnic.

Only she hadn't been there.

She would never be there again.

She was lying on a cold slab in a cold morgue.

I took the letter over to the fireplace and held a match beneath it. It was reluctant to burn; I had to light three more matches to accomplish it: or maybe it was just my shaking hands.

I could do that much for her.

No need for a bunch of nosy cops to know that her old man only got drunk on Saturday nights now.

No, no need.

I sat down on the bed and jiggled up and down on the mattress. It was quiet. It had seemed to me, the night before, that it had been making enough noise to rouse the whole neighborhood.

I lay back down on the bed and covered my face with my hands and said to myself, cut it out, cut it out, cut it out, Phelan. Get up and walk through that door and leave. Let someone else stick their nose into the dirt and the grime. Go away. Run away. It's nothing. Don't think about it. To hell with the negatives; to hell with who killed Memo Sanchez and Jean Gibbon and Cock Robin, and to hell with everything else, too; let the bodies fall where they may. It's none of your concern. She was cheap at the price and she did a lot of things that make you sick at your stomach: and what the hell kind of a jerk are you? You're a tough guy, Phelan; you've got a reputation for beating up old ladies. Things like this don't bother you; hell, no.

I picked myself up from the bed and let my emotions wring themselves dry. All right.

I walked over to the dresser. I had a job to do. Various cosmetics lay around in various positions; all the usual stuff. I picked up a bottle of perfume and sniffed at it; it was familiar, nice and familiar. I opened the top drawer of the dresser. Undies, bras, slips, nothing that thrilled me much. And then I saw a small stack of papers tucked away in one corner. I lifted them out of the drawer and took a closer look at them. There were about a dozen of them, folded in half. It was light blue writing paper, heavy and expensive like some men use. I opened one of them and read the typewriting inside:

> Darling: You are the most beautiful thing in the world. I love you.

It was unsigned.

I opened another one. It read:

> Darling: I bought five more photos of you from M. You are divine. I dream of you, I think of you constantly. I go to sleep each night with you staring down at me, loving me, too. I adore you. I love you.

It, also, was unsigned.

The others were much the same, brief messages of adoration, a peculiar type of adoration. Gush. I could picture some poor little sap sitting in some tawdry little room, night after night, banging out these notes on his typewriter, the photographs of Jean near by, his mind twisting around something, turning it from a clean, wholesome matter of nature into a dirty, sordid matter of the mind.

I read them all over again and then sat down and read them a third time. Something clicked in the back of my mind. I had an idea; it was the first one in a long time, but at least it was a start.

I put them all back in the drawer. The police could have them; they could play with them, as I was going to do.

And then I walked back into the living room, letting that idea mull around in the back of my head.

There was one of those special little pamphlets for telephone numbers near the phone; I picked it up and went through it.

There were two numbers in it; the first number I dialed gave me the time; the second number was the Atlas Cleaners.

I gave that up, and stood there looking at the phone. I dialed one more number.

"Dr. Margolis' office."

"Dr. Margolis, please."

"Who's calling?"

"John J. Phelan."

"Just a moment, please."

There was a silence, and then: "Dr. Margolis speaking."

"Doctor, this is John J. Phelan. I'm a private investigator working for Mr. J. Walter Pendleton. His wife, I am told, is a patient of yours."

"Yes?"

"Mr. Pendleton hired me because he thinks his wife's life is in danger. He tells me that she has been suffering from a serious heart ailment for a number of years. I'd like to know exactly how sick she is."

"You know I can't answer that, Mr. Phelan. Especially not over the telephone."

"I can come to your office."

"I'm afraid that wouldn't do you any good. Mr. Pendleton is not my patient; his wife is, that's true. I'm not in a position to divulge the seriousness or lack of same of any illness of any of my patients. As a private investigator, Mr. Phelan, you should be aware of that fact."

"I am aware of it, Dr. Margolis. But under the circumstances—"

"What circumstances?"

"I told you. We think, both Mr. Pendleton and myself, that his wife's life is in danger. Someone might be trying to murder her."

"Just a moment," he said.

It was a long moment. I stood there and winked at one of the pale little ballerinas; I was almost certain that she winked back. We were having a gay old time when Dr. Margolis finally returned.

"All right, Mr. Phelan," he said. "Please continue."

"There's nothing to continue, Dr. Margolis. I told you what I wanted. I would appreciate your cooperation, but I can't force you to give it to me."

"No," he said, "you can't. Just what makes you think someone is trying to murder Mrs. Pendleton?"

I hesitated a moment. "She supposedly has a very weak heart. If my information on that is correct, someone might be trying to shock her into an attack."

"That's ridiculous."

"I'm glad you think so."

I waited, and waited some more.

"I'm sorry, Mr. Phelan," he said after another long silence, "that I could not be of more help to you."

"Someone else," I said, "might be more sorry later on."

We hung up on each other. He'd been a lot of help.

I took one more swing around the apartment. I don't know what I expected to find, maybe Jean Gibbon's ghost. The only thing that happened was that that pale little ballerina gave me the eye on my way out.

Adam Wheeler was waiting for me outside the building. He was leaning up against the fender of his car, his arms crossed over his thin chest, his mouth working overtime on a piece of gum. He looked as if he had been waiting for some time.

I said: "Thanks a lot, Adam."

He shrugged, and said: "Find anything?"

"Nothing interesting."

"If Lundeberg finds out I let you up there first, my tail won't be worth a plugged nickel."

"I said thanks, Adam."

"I know you did."

"Did you see the body?"

"Yes." He nodded, and looked at me. "She was dead before she hit the water. Strangled."

"Anything else?"

He thought about that. "You mean like rape?"

"I mean like rape."

"No," he said, "not that. But she was given a pretty good beating. There were bruises all over her shoulders, breasts, thighs, and stomach."

"Goddamn," I said.

He straightened upright. He spit the gum out on the curbing, then took out a cigarette, lighting it.

He said: "I can't figure the connection with the Sanchez thing. It's got to be there, somewhere, but I can't figure it, not right now. The girl looked as if she had been had by a sick mind, Johnny, a damned sick mind."

"Shut up, for Chrissakes," I said.

I started to walk away. He grabbed me by the arm.

"Johnny, don't do anything foolish. I've stuck my neck way out in this thing, trying to help you. I won't again. I know that girl touched you inside, and I know what kind of a goose you are. Don't take it on yourself to fix the whole thing. I'll say one thing about her, nothing more. She was a tramp, pure and simple, no better than any other broad that ever posed for that kind of pictures." He stopped; he was breathing hard. He looked down at my hands, and I followed his gaze; my hands were knotted up into fists. "That's all, Johnny. Beat it."

Sure, beat it.

That's just what I did: and why not?

CHAPTER TWELVE

IDLED the Dodge down to the corner on Sunset, waiting there for the light to change. I glanced in the rear-view mirror, more out of habit than anything else. Adam Wheeler was just going into the apartment building. A tan Chevvie coupe pulled out from the curb half a block up the hill, behind me. The light winked green. I turned right, west, on Sunset. I saw the tan Chevvie coupe swing around the corner and come in the same direction.

Coincidence? Maybe.

I continued west on Sunset for about a mile, then turned south; the Chevvie kept pace. I cut back east on Santa Monica, heading for my apartment; still, the Chevvie kept coming.

Whoever it was driving that Chevvie was either awfully new at the tailing business or he or she didn't mind that I knew someone was following me. Or maybe they thought I was just plain dumb: and maybe they weren't too far wrong. I didn't care; not then.

I parked in front of my apartment building and sat there for a moment, letting the motor idle. I finally cut it off and stepped out into the street. The tan Chevvie coupe was double-parked about fifty yards up the street.

I debated on whether or not to brazen it out and walk up to the Chevvie. But I was unarmed. It could be the rough boys again, back for some more laughter and good times. If that was so, I wanted an even break.

I went on up to my apartment. Mrs. Harding, the manager, had cleaned it again and, as usual, had closed all the blinds. She seemed to have a personal gripe against sunlight, or what passes for it in Los Angeles. I crossed to the window, opening one of the venetian blinds. Sunlight bounced in and found a resting place.

I looked out the window. The tan Chevvie coupe was still there, still double-parked. Finally, a girl got out. She leaned against the Chevvie for a moment, resting one hand against the closed door, balancing herself; then she walked stiff-legged, body bent forward, the way some drunks do when they're concentrating everything they've got on reaching a certain point, and disappeared below me into the building entrance.

The Chevvie eased past the building and turned at the corner. I got the license number, 2N3831, which proved that I had at least some of my senses still left.

I opened another venetian blind and let in some more sunlight; it joined the other.

Then I went over to the door and opened it, and waited, and it wasn't a long wait.

Honor Pendleton was somewhere along on a real first-class binge; she smelled like twenty-year-old Scotch whiskey and her eyes had the glazed, fixed look that made it seem she had been that way for a couple of days. Her makeup was smeared and in the wrong places, giving her a lop-sided, crazy-quilted kind of appearance.

She looked at me, taking a long time to focus properly, giggled, and tweaked me under the chin. She clutched an expensive leather purse up under her chin and said, "Lover boy."

I let her brush by me into the apartment. She put everything she owned right against me and pushed, but I wasn't taking any of it. I stepped out into the hallway and had my look; no one else was about.

I went back in and closed the door behind me. She was standing in the middle of the room, swaying dangerously at varying angles; her tongue came out, searching for something it couldn't find, and she giggled again. Her knees buckled, quite suddenly, and she tumbled to the floor.

I went over and picked her up. She locked her arms behind my neck and gave me the pushing business again; I still wasn't taking any of it. I broke her hold and half-pushed her into a chair.

She said, "Lover boy" again, and then reached over, picking up the purse she had dropped near the chair. I held my breath, wondering if she would make it. I was through helping her. She got it, finally. She straightened up, falling back into the chair, repeated that "lover boy" thing for the third time, and then laughed hysterically. The laughter bounced around in the room, pushing at me.

She was poured into her dress, but only up to a certain point. Or points. A necklace of what seemed like real pearls adorned her pretty neck. The skirt had lifted itself high. Maybe she had planned it that way, but I wasn't interested.

She looked down at the purse clutched before her and the laughter fell back into that monotonous giggle again. She opened the purse: and the thing she pointed at me made me as scared as hell. I hadn't figured on that, not at all. A gun in the hands of a drunk, especially a woman drunk, is no laughing matter, and I wasn't laughing.

She waved the gun at me and kept on giggling and something moved up from my belly and stuck right in my throat. I had had it before. It was fear.

I said one word: "Why?"

But she just kept on giggling.

I took one step to the side, then two straight ahead, toward her. She blinked her eyes, stopped the giggling momentarily, and chewed on her lips; she blinked again, and the words came through her teeth. "You caused a lotta trouble." I had a hard time making them out; she slurred them together, but I got the idea.

She hiccoughed. It probably saved my life, because I jumped forward just at that moment and slapped the gun aside; she dropped it to the floor. I put my foot on it. The necklace had parted, scattering pearls all over the floor. Between her and the pearls, that floor had never had it so good. She sat there and looked down at the gun, then up at me, giggled again and again, blinked again and again, and then told me to do something to myself that I don't like to do.

I hit her right on the point of her chin.

She slumped down without a sound.

I went into the kitchen and got out the bottle of bourbon from the cabinet. It took two long swigs to chase away that feeling from the back of my neck. I took a third swig, just to be on the safe side.

I went back into the living room and over to the window to have another look-see outside. The tan Chevvie hadn't returned. I didn't figure that; that would take a little time. I turned around. The gun still lay on the floor where she had dropped it. I walked over and picked it up. It was a .38 revolver, Smith & Wesson make; the serial number had not been scratched off. I broke it open, looking inside. All the shells were in place. It was pearl-handled, and there was a small nick on the left side of the handle, marring its smoothness.

I put the gun in my coat pocket, then took off my coat and hung it on the back of a chair.

I looked down at Honor Pendleton. That name, *Honor*. That gave me a laugh. Her head was lying at a crazy angle over the arm of the chair. A bruise was slowly darkening over her chin where I had hit her.

I didn't feel sorry for her.

I went over to the phone book and searched through it for Jean Gibbon's number; I found it, and dialed it.

Adam Wheeler answered.

I said: "Adam, what—"

He didn't let me get any further. "You bastard. You real, first-class, A-number-one bastard."

"What's eating you?"

"You said you didn't find anything here."

"And I didn't."

"What do you think I am?" He didn't wait for my answer. "A Boy Scout could tell you just burned something in the fireplace. Fresh ashes. I wish they were yours."

I had forgotten about that letter. "It wasn't anything, Adam. Nothing at all."

"I wish you would've let me decide that."

"I will, next time."

"Yeah. Next time. There might not be a next time." He paused. "What was it you burned?"

"It was a letter from the girl's mother. It didn't amount to a hill of beans in this case, just said that her old man got drunk on Saturday nights now and not seven days a week." He didn't say anything, and neither did I for another minute. Then: "Has the gun that killed Sanchez been found?"

"Why?"

"I was just wondering."

"Well, wonder some more. I'm through helping you."

"Come on, Adam, answer the question."

"I wish you'd remember one sweet little goddamned fact of life, Mr. John J. Phelan. I'm the cop around here. I get paid for this, not you."

I didn't say anything. He cleared his throat uncomfortably.

"No," he said, finally, "the gun hasn't been found."

"Then maybe I've got a present for you."

"Such as the murder gun?"

"Could be. It's a wild guess, but it's the most I've had in a long time. It's worth the play. Why don't you come over here and pick it up?"

"Where'd you get it?"

"I'll tell you that when you get here."

"You'll probably need the time to think up a story. I'll be there in fifteen minutes."

"One other thing."

"What's that? My right arm?"

"Check a license number for me. A fifty-one Chevvie, number 2N3831."

He repeated the number after me, then said: "And is that all the Los Angeles police force can do for you today, Mr. Phelan?"

I laughed at him, and hung up.

But I wasn't laughing at myself.

I took a look at Honor Pendleton; she hadn't gone any place. I sat down and watched her for some five minutes, letting an idea go round and round in my mind. I tried to figure out what it was that made her tick, but it was a hopeless situation. Finally, I went over and picked her up and carried her into the bedroom and deposited her on the bed. She groaned once, and then was silent. She had passed from the unconsciousness of a knockout into the deep slumber of a drunk. I got a pair of old handcuffs from a bureau drawer; I put one of them around her right wrist and the other one around the post of the bed: just in case.

Then I picked up all the pearls from the floor in the other room, put them in her bag, threw the bag on the bed next to her.

I closed the bedroom door behind me. No need for Wheeler to know what was in there. I took the gun out of my coat pocket and rubbed it clean of all fingerprints with my handkerchief. I put the gun down on the floor near the chair in which she had sat.

I went back into the kitchen. I had just finished mixing two tall glasses of bourbon and water when the buzzer sounded. I carried the drinks with me and went to answer the door.

Adam Wheeler's face was sour, as sour as I had ever seen it. A line ran down from his forehead on to the beginnings of his long nose; I had seen that line a couple of times before: he was dangerously near the breaking point. He opened his mouth to speak, but I shoved the drink at him.

"My buy," I said.

He hesitated. He looked at the drink I held out to him, then at me, then back at the drink. He took the drink, considered it for a moment, then swallowed half of it in one gulp.

I turned around, and he followed me into the apartment. He saw the gun on the floor immediately, as I had known he would. He stooped down, looking at it; he put his glass down on the rug, took out a long yellow pencil from his inner coat pocket, put that through the trigger guard of the gun, and lifted the gun up to sniff at its barrel. It was standard procedure. He looked up at me, scowled for the tenth time since he had entered the room, and then wrapped the gun in a handkerchief and put it in his coat pocket. He finished the drink without rising.

He was a cop then, a cop with a cop's inborn distaste for anything out of the ordinary.

"A pretty little thing," he said, rising.

I nodded.

He said: "You've stretched things a long way between us, Johnny. I don't know, maybe too long. I know we've been through a lot together. I'm way up the creek with you and the paddle was lost long ago. But god damn you, if you're playing games with me. I'll stick it to you, believe me, I will."

I believed him.

I took the first sip of my drink, and shuddered; things were piling up on me, too high and too fast. I was getting in the corner with no way out.

I got his glass and went into the kitchen and fixed him another drink. He was still standing there when I came back out and handed him the drink. He twirled the glass around in his long fingers and looked at nothing in particular.

I sat down, and he did likewise. We didn't look at each other; we let the silence pile up between us, each with his own thoughts and memories. I knew that's what he was doing: remembering. I was counting on it. He took a couple of short jolts from his drink, then put the glass down. He removed his hat and scratched at his thinning hair.

"Damn dandruff," he said. "Drives me nuts. I've tried seventy-seven different cures for it. None of 'em worked. Not one."

I didn't say anything.

He said: "I suppose you're going to tell me you walked in here and found the gun lying on the floor and, like all good, law-abiding citizens, you immediately called me to report this fact."

I nodded.

"Crap," he said. "What about that license number?"

"Someone's been tailing me. I want to know who it is."

"Uh-huh," he said. "And what'll I tell Lundeberg when I bring this gun in, providing it is the murder weapon?"

"Tell him the truth, Adam." I smiled, but not very big; I wasn't feeling very big right then. "The truth is mightier than—"

"Cut it out."

I did.

"Lundeberg'll roast you," he said. "Maybe me, too."

"You can take care of yourself, Adam. I know that, or I wouldn't try this on you. As for me, let him try me on for size. I'm clean."

"Are you clean, Johnny?"

"You're worried about that letter I burned, Adam. Don't be. I swear it had nothing to do with this case. It said some things about a church picnic and some other things about her drunken old man and I didn't want anyone else to read it. I was a sap; I admit it."

"That's right," he said. "You were. Maybe you still are."

"Remember the Alamo," I said, and forced a smile. I was forcing everything now.

"You sonofabitch," he said. "Don't bring up that buddy-buddy crap with me. The war's been over for ten years."

"Sure," I said.

He finished his drink, stood up, and stretched his long arms towards the ceiling. He took a look at the closed door leading to my bedroom. He frowned, scratched at his head again, and then clamped on his hat.

He said, "I'll check this gun. I see the serial number is still on it. Maybe it's registered. Stranger things have happened. But I'm going to tell Lundeberg just what happened, Johnny. I'm going to give him the truth. I'm not sticking my neck out any further. I've got a wife and kids. You're on your own from now on."

"Hell," I said, "you'll probably get a promotion out of this."

"I don't want any damn promotion. I got enough problems now." He walked to the door. "I'll call you about the license number."

After he had gone a few minutes, I went over to the phone and got The Red Barn in Dorsett. I asked for Miss Lannie Dixon. My phone bill had increased by the time she came on.

I said: "This is John J. Phelan."

"How thrilling."

"You'd better get over to my apartment as soon as you can. You know the way. Your kid sister's here, drunker than hell. She's trying to rape me. I may weaken at any moment."

She gasped, just before I hung up.

CHAPTER THIRTEEN

I LAY in the bathtub and let the warm water grow cool around me. A whole army of little green men with heads shaped like eggs came out of the faucet, swam up the length of the tub, and deposited something dirty and heavy on my chest. I made a half-hearted attempt at fending them off, but there were too many of them.

I gave up.

Water seeping into my sinking nose awakened me. I sat upright, a shock running through me. I had almost fallen asleep in the bathtub.

I got out of the tub, dried myself carefully, and walked into the bedroom. Honor Pendleton didn't blush. She didn't do anything. She was still drifting along in her own peculiar channel, unaware of the vicious everyday world, unaware of all the trouble she had brought about.

I put on a clean T-shirt and had just finished inspecting a couple of new gray hairs when the buzzer sounded. My apartment was getting to be as busy as Hollywood and Vine.

I slipped into a pair of brown gabardine pants, patted the one curl I own into place, and went out to answer the door.

Landrith Pendleton's face had a strained, almost ghastly look about it. It had aged considerably since the last time I had seen it.

I jerked a thumb over my shoulder and said: "She's in there. You know the way."

She hardly looked at me. She brushed quickly by and dashed into the bedroom. I went over to the phone and dialed a number.

I ordered three ham-and-swiss sandwiches on Russian rye and a bottle of Budweiser from Louie's delicatessen on the corner.

I hung up, and went into the bedroom. Landrith Pendleton was sitting on the edge of the bed, her back to her sister, staring down at the floor. She was wearing dark blue toreador pants and a white blouse, sleeveless, and buttoned high on her throat. Her hands hung down limply between her knees.

She looked up at me briefly, but the look was meaningless. I flexed my muscles at her, but nothing happened. I went over to the bureau, got a cigarette, lit it, then walked back over to hand it her. She inhaled deeply, keeping the smoke in her lungs; she wasn't worried about a little thing like cancer: not then.

She said, "Was all this necessary?"

"All what?"

"The bruise on her chin. The handcuffs."

"I had to protect my virtue in some way."

"Don't try to be funny. This isn't a funny thing with me."

"It's not funny with me either, sweetheart. She came in here waving a gun in my direction, hating me for some reason I don't know, tanked to the gills."

"She's a lot of things, this one." She shook her head and looked away from me. "She's just a poor kid, Phelan, a poor, mixed-up kid who doesn't know right from wrong. No one ever took the time to teach her that."

"She knows," I said. "I had a talk with her a long, long time ago. She said then that everyone excused her actions. She asked me not to do that. I just obliged her. She could just as easily have killed me as not. I don't care how mixed-up or how poor she is, she knew damned good and well that was wrong."

"You're a sweet fellow, Phelan," she said.

She took two quick puffs on the cigarette, then looked around for an ashtray. She spotted the one on the bedside table. Her breasts pushed tautly against the blouse as she made the long reach. I went over and got out a clean shirt and put it on. I took the key and unlocked the handcuffs. Honor Pendleton stirred slightly, but didn't open her eyes.

"Well," said Landrith Pendleton, "now what?"

"How come you hate your father so?"

She studied a fingernail; she studied it for a long time and I could barely hear her words. "You mean Walter, don't you? I don't hate Walter. I don't hate him at all. I don't feel anything toward him. Nothing."

I was just wondering who else she thought I had meant when the phone in the living room began ringing. I hustled out to answer it. It was Adam Wheeler. His voice was curiously taut.

"The gun checks out, Johnny," he said. "Ballistics matched it up with the slugs taken from Memo Sanchez."

"Both of them?"

"Yeah. The gun is registered to a Landrith Pendleton. We're chasing her down now. Know her?"

"Never heard of her."

"How you can lie, Johnny. How you can lie."

"Sure," I said. "It comes easy. Did you check the license number for me?"

"Car's registered to a Neal H. Leggett, 4211 Melrose. Oh-oh, here comes Lundeberg. The storm flag's up."

I started to hang up, but Lundeberg's angry voice jumped at me over the wire. "Phelan? Is that you, Phelan?"

"I cannot tell a lie," I said.

"Listen, you wise-cracking no-good, I want some answers out of you, some damned good answers and damned quick. I'm sending a squad car out to pick you up." Just as he said that, I heard a police siren in the distance, coming from the direction of the Hollywood Freeway; its wail was shrill and lonely, and it was increasing. "You come downtown with the boys. I'm going to teach you not to interfere with police business."

"Bye bye, baby," I said, and hung up.

The phone began ringing again, almost immediately. I let it. The siren was picking up volume. I went back into the bedroom. Landrith Pendleton had her sister sitting up on the edge of the bed and was washing her face with a cold towel. Honor looked at me briefly, blinking her eyes.

The siren continued to grow.

"The police are coming here," I said. "They'll be here any minute. We'd better get out of here."

Landrith Pendleton said: "I'm not running from the police. I've got nothing to hide."

"Suit yourself, sweetheart." I said. "The gun your kid sister there was poking at me is in the hands of the police. It's the same gun that rid the world of one Memo Sanchez. It also happens to be registered in your name. You can sit here and debate the issue with them if you want. I'm leaving."

The siren wasn't more than six blocks away now, growing larger every second.

The two sisters didn't hesitate much. Honor moved with surprising swiftness for one in her condition, and I thought I knew the reason for this. I locked the door behind us, and we went down the back steps just as the siren gave out with its final little yelp in front of the building. We came out in the alley. Honor stumbled against something, falling to the ground, knocking over a garbage can; bottles and cans rattled to the pavement. I picked her up. I looked down the alley towards the front of the building. I could see Bennie, Louie's kid, slumping along with a sack in his hand; he turned his head just at that moment, catching sight of me. I motioned him to go back and he caught on: a bright boy, that one; I'd have to remember that.

"Where's your car?" I asked Landrith.

"On the corner, out front," she said.

"All right. Go get it. Walk right out in front like nothing happened. Go slow and easy, act natural. Drive around the block and meet us at the other end of the alley. Go on."

I took Honor by the arm, holding her close to me, as Landrith moved briskly toward the street. Honor and I hugged close to the garages, walking rapidly down the alley; I didn't think we could be seen from upstairs, but I wasn't sure. I turned around once, just in time to see Landrith turn the corner of the building. She didn't look back.

The bath hadn't done me much good. The sun was shining in the distance, but it was still hot. I was sweating right through my clean clothes. Honor Pendleton suddenly wasn't much help; she began dragging her feet. All the quick movements, the suddenness of the hot afternoon sun, made her sick. We stopped, and she vomited against the rear-end of a Studebaker jutting out from a garage. Someone would be madder than hell. I could have vomited myself without too much trouble.

And why was I running away? I wasn't guilty of anything. Just withholding evidence from the police. They could take my license and throw it into the Pacific Ocean; maybe they would.

A lime-green Ford Thunderbird with the top down moved into the opening of the street ahead of us. Landrith Pendleton waved hesitantly. I half-carried Honor the rest of the way. I went around on the right side of the car and shoved her into the seat; then, I went back around and pushed Landrith into the middle, getting behind the wheel myself.

I spared no rubber getting out of there.

It wasn't my rubber anyway.

CHAPTER FOURTEEN

DROVE OVER to Vermont and then turned north into Griffith Park. The picnic-lovers were just leaving, and the sex-lovers were just arriving; it was that time of day. We went past the Greek Theatre. The Thunderbird climbed the winding hill road with ease; I had quite a car beneath me. We came out by the observatory, and I found a parking space. A touring bus loaded with eager eyes backed up, scratching the rear fender of the Thunderbird; the driver stopped the bus. He got out, looked at me, at the Thunderbird, and waited for me to say something. I didn't, so he got back in and went off on his tour.

The city lay below us, spread out like a jigsaw puzzle. The sun bounced off the dense smog and hurt my eyes. Cars were tiny little animals crawling up and down the long thin streams of black below us. Two teen-age girls in tight-fitting sweaters with swinging hips pranced by; they were almost goosing each other in their joy. A young punk with a ducktail haircut and a badge of yellowheaded pimples on his forehead sauntered by after them, licking his lips.

Life went on.

I lit a cigarette and let my heart go back down where it belonged. Honor Pendleton opened the door on her side and dry-retched over the paving. The sound choked me, too. I slammed my hand, suddenly, against the dashboard. That accomplished a great big fat nothing. I only got a sore hand out of it.

Landrith Pendleton said: "I wish—"

I cut her short: "I don't give a damn what you wish. Just shut up and sit there."

Her mouth opened and closed, and she shuddered, almost as if she were cold. Her lips set themselves in a prim line and she folded her hands in her lap.

Honor Pendleton got out of the car. She stumbled across the narrow sidewalk and collapsed in the brief shade of a peeling eucalyptus tree. She looked almost human; almost.

I said: "I'm sorry I blew up. I'm just tight inside, all worked up. I don't know from nothing."

"No," Landrith Pendleton said, "don't be sorry. We're the ones who should be that, not you. It's all such a mess, such a horrible, horrible mess." She turned to look at me, revealing a softness behind her eyes that looked real. "The police were out this morning. I...I'm truly sorry about Miss Gibbon. It must be difficult for you."

Sure, that was it. Difficult. In a nutshell.

"I knew her for, maybe, six hours."

"Oh?"

The kid with the pimples and the haircut walked by again. Apparently, he had failed with the goose-girls; or maybe he hadn't even tried. He didn't look like the type who would give it an honest try. He spotted Honor lying on the grass, her dress above her kness. He paused in his walking. His greedy little eyes moved up and down and around and something that passed for a tongue came out and flicked over his thick, pinkish lips. He stuck his hands deep down in his pockets and rocked back and forth: he was having himself quite a time.

I stuck my head out the window and said: "Beat it, bub. It's not for sale."

He whirled around to stare at me. He murmured, "Who wants to buy, smart guy?" and then his lips formed an obscenity about what I could do to myself, but he didn't have the guts to say it out loud. He kicked out at the sidewalk, and then idled in low gear on up toward the observatory, looking for something else at which he could stare and dream.

"I'm real tough," I said. "With kids."

She kept silent.

"What about that gun?" I asked.

"What about it?"

"I told you, back at my place. You were listening. The gun that killed Memo Sanchez, the one your sister was pointing at me, the one that supposedly belongs to you. It's registered in your name."

"What am I supposed to say?"

"Anything that comes into your mind. Try the truth."

"You make it sound like the truth is something all wrapped up in a pretty little package with a blue bow around it. I don't know what the truth is. I'm beginning to think I don't know what anything is, any more."

"I'd like to know more about your father."

She studied my face, carefully.

"You questioned me about him before. Why?"

"Just something in the back of my mind."

"Well, leave it there. I won't answer any questions about him."

"Will you answer any questions at all?"

She lifted her shoulders in a helpless little gesture. And then she did something that surprised the hell out of me. I was prepared for almost anything but that. She began crying and sobbing, and it was good, and it was believable. Only it didn't fit her, somehow. She leaned over and rested her face against my shoulder; you know, that shoulder that's big enough for the whole world to cry on. It was certainly getting a good workout.

I just sat there and let her cry, and watched her sister. Honor staggered to her feet. She looked up toward the sky and sucked in some air. She looked all around her, apparently reorienting herself back into humanity. She came across the short space and leaned her head in the car window, resting it on her forearms.

She looked more dead than alive. She watched Landrith's sobbing for some time, then said: "Christ, I've got a head on me." She raised weary eyes in my direction. "I've really done it this time," she said, "haven't I?"

"Exactly what have you done?"

Her head bobed up and down. She reached out with a tender hand to touch her sister lightly on the thigh.

"You know, Phelan," she said. "You know."

"Why did you try to kill me?"

The shock seemed genuine. "You, too?"

"Yeah," I said.

"Oh, my God," murmured Landrith into my shoulder.

"I had to kill him, honey," said Honor. "Honest, I did. Honest to God. He was no good; he was rotten clear through to his yellow backbone. Just too much happened, that's all. Just too much happened."

I was listening, but I wasn't hearing much. Not much.

"Okay," I said, "get in the car. Let's get out of here."

Honor got in the car. She dropped her head against the back of the seat and closed her eyes and, I suppose, went back to her own private little world, a world of alcohol and sex and perversion and millions of dollars.

Landrith turned tear-wet eyes to me, and the question was there.

"No," I said, "not to the police. Not yet."

CHAPTER FIFTEEN

I swung the Thunderbird around and headed back down the hill toward Hollywood. I turned east toward Cahuenga and got jumbled in with all the five o'clock traffic and finally found a motel with a vacancy sign out front.

Neither girl had spoken during the short drive. Honor hadn't even bothered to open her eyes. The two had ridden along, mute and motionless as a couple of dummies.

I registered as Earl Moore and the old lady with the tired brown hair and the plump red face showed us to our cottage. Suspicion showed all over her face and then, when she got a whiff of Honor, the suspicion changed abruptly to disgust. She started to say something, then thought better of it as I paid in advance.

The three of us went into the cottage. It was dark and almost dank inside. Honor fell down on one of the beds, taking a comfortable position on her stomach. Landrith went into the bathroom and closed the door behind her.

I stood at the window, peeped through the closed blinds and saw the tired brown hair disappear into her office. The traffic crept along on the crowded freeway, so many giant bugs being pushed along from behind. Guys going home to their wives and kids and televisions and arguments.

I heard Landrith coming out of the bathroom. She clicked on a light. I turned around. Honor moaned, and flopped over on her back. Landrith's face looked scrubbed and clean.

"I'd better get some food," I said. "I'll be back in no more than twenty minutes. Don't either one of you leave here or make a phone call."

Landrith nodded, slumping down in a chair with bamboo arms and legs.

I left them, drove back the short distance into downtown Hollywood, stopped at the first restaurant I came to. I ordered six hamburgers and three quarts of buttermilk. There was a pay phone on one wall of the restaurant; I used it. The man I talked to had been an extra in *Birth of a Nation*. He had also been an extra in just about every picture made since that time. He knew almost everything about everyone in the film world, and what he didn't know off-hand, he could find out. It would cost, but it was worth it. What I wanted to learn, right then, he wasn't sure about; he told me he thought he could get the information in a couple of hours. I told him I would call back.

The shower was running in the bathroom when I returned to the motel cottage. Landrith told me that Honor was in there cleaning up.

There were only two chairs in the room, the bamboo thing near the bathroom door, and a round-backed reed chair in the corner. I sat down in the reed chair and began work on a hamburger and a quart of buttermilk. I was hungry. Landrith pecked hesitantly at a hamburger but turned her nose up at the buttermilk. We ate in silence. I had nothing to say to her; not then.

After a while, Honor came out of the bathroom. She hadn't bothered to dress, instead had wrapped herself in a big bath towel. It was large enough to cover most of her, but my mind was on too many other things at that moment to much care, one way or the other.

Honor didn't want the buttermilk or the hamburgers. I didn't force her to eat, but I did force her to drink the buttermilk. She made a lot of dirty faces doing it, but she finally managed to finish a whole quart. That's all I could ask. I wanted her settled and sober, or as settled and sober as she could possibly get.

The single light wasn't much. I sat mostly in darkness, listening to the steady hum of traffic outside, watching the two girls. Honor took a position on the bed, lying on her side, resting her head in an upturned palm, staring at me.

"Okay," I said, finally, "let's begin."

"What is there to begin?" This from Landrith.

"You both know that your father hired me last Saturday. You both know the reason he did so. Since that day, two people have been murdered. I want to fit some of the pieces together. Time is getting short. The police are breathing down our necks, and our necks are pretty far out."

"*Our* necks, Phelan?" Again, it was Landrith.

"*Our* necks, sweetheart," I said. "I'm going to ask some questions and I want some damned good answers. I don't want any amateur dramatics. I'm up to my ears in trouble, running off from the police like that. I've got to do something and be quick about it. It doesn't take much to get my license revoked—maybe I've already gone too far. I hope you both appreciate that fact."

Maybe they did; they didn't say no.

"First," I went on, looking at Honor, "you said up at the observatory that you had had to kill *him*. By him, I take it, you meant Memo Sanchez."

She murmured a soft, "Yes."

"I want to know how and when and under what circumstances."

Honor shook her head. She sat up, and opened and closed her mouth and looked up at the ceiling.

"Okay," I said, "if that's the way it's going to be. I'll call the police. I'll ride the thing through that way. We'll see what happens."

I sat there and slowly counted to thirty. Landrith rose and crossed over to sit on the bed beside her sister. The towel came loose, baring some of Honor's charms. No one seemed to notice, me least of all.

I shrugged. I got to my feet and lifted the phone.

Landrith spoke behind my back: "You'd better tell him, honey. He means it."

There was no reply.

I picked up the receiver.

"Wait a minute." It was Honor. She added, "Please."

I turned around, holding the receiver in my hand.

"I'll tell you," she said. Her voice broke a little. "It isn't easy, you know."

"I don't know anything," I said.

Landrith gave me a sharp, hurt look.

I ignored the look, replaced the receiver and sat down again in the reed chair.

Honor's voice was barely above a whisper. "It—it's sort of vague. I didn't know about Memo sending those pictures to mother until late Friday. I really didn't. I never dreamed anything like that would happen. I found out about it quite by accident. I was in—well, in Memo's bedroom Friday night. Sleeping off a jag. When I woke up, someone was arguing with Memo out in the front room. I was still hazy and had a horrible head, but I lay there and caught a few of the words, enough to add the whole thing together." She grinned a helpless little grin, for the first time looking her true age. "Anyway, Memo was arguing with Leggett—"

I interrupted: "Who's Leggett?"

"Neal Leggett. He worked with Memo. He's a photographer."

"Go on."

"I got up and went to the door and listened. They were really going at it hot and heavy. Leggett has a horrible temper, and they were arguing about the pictures they'd sent to mother. God, I didn't know." She turned to her sister. "Honest, Lannie, I didn't. I never would've done it. I'm low, I know, but not that low."

Landrith said: "It's all right, honey, it's all right."

I was glad she thought so.

Honor shuddered; she wrapped her arms around her middle and said: "God, I need a drink."

"You won't get one," I said.

She buried her face in her hands, very dramatically; she was good at it. Landrith got up, lighting a cigarette with jerky hands, gave it to her sister. Honor puffed quickly, and then threw the cigarette across the room. It hit the wall and sputtered down to the rug. I watched it die a natural death. I waited the whole thing out. Finally, Honor got hold of herself a bit.

She said, "I went into the front room. Memo tried to cover up what they'd been arguing about, but I'd have none of that. I blew up at them. Leggett seemed to side with me. I don't know why, but he did. Memo turned on him and they had a fight. It wasn't much of a battle. Leggett was too old and too fat, and Memo threw him out of the apartment. And then he got on me. He said a lot of dirty things, things that were true, I guess. He called me a lot of cheap names and said there was no reason in the world why my mother should have so much money and he should have so little. He scared me so much that I ran from the apartment."

"Were you dressed?"

"Not fully, but enough. Leggett was downstairs. I cried on his shoulder, and he was sweet to me. He took me to a little apartment I keep on the Strip and I got some clothes. I—I did the only thing I know how to do in such emergencies—I got good and stinking drunk. I remember a lot of bars and a lot of different people, and Leggett was always with me. Oh, I got drunk—you can't imagine how drunk I got. I wanted to blot out everything, but just everything. I remember waking up some time Saturday and I was completely naked and"—if I hadn't known better, I would have sworn she blushed at that—"and Leggett was still there. I guess we were in his apartment; it was dirty and shoddy. He told me the whole thing, how Memo was trying to blackmail mother by sending her those pictures of me. I wanted to kill Memo right then, I did. But Leggett told me you were in on it, you and Memo and Walter all together. I believed him. He said Walter had given you the originals and that maybe I could get them from you. He sobered me up a little, and then I went over to visit you. You remember?"

I nodded.

"But you wouldn't cooperate," she said. "After seeing you, I went out and got drunk again. There didn't seem to be anything else to do, not then. And all I can recall after that is going up to Memo's apartment and seeing him there and shooting him. I killed him. I killed him. God, I didn't know what I was doing—"

She was wringing her hands and her eyes had a blank look.

"Fine," I said. "Take it easy. It's over now."

"Is it?" asked Landrith.

I gave Honor a couple of more minutes to come back to this world, then asked: "Do you have any idea of what the time was when you shot Memo?"

She shook her head.

"Where'd you get the gun?"

Again, she shook her head.

"Come on, where'd you get it?"

"It was Lannie's."

"I know that. But how did you get it?"

Once more, she shook her head.

I looked at Landrith; she, too, shook her head.

"Look," I said, "I've got to know about that gun."

"If it is my gun," said Landrith, "I bought it about a year ago. Some creep was following me home every night, and I bought it for protection. I kept it at my apartment."

"When was the last time you saw it?"

"I don't know for sure. I kept it in a box in the closet. Maybe—oh, I don't know—months ago."

"I stole it," announced Honor.

"When?"

"I don't know. Can't you understand that? I have no idea of time, none whatsoever. Days pass, weeks pass. I just know that she had a gun and I had a key to her apartment and Leggett said—"

"Leggett was with you at the time?"

"I guess so. Yes. I remember it was before I came over here to see you. Leggett and I were talking about what we could do—he had agreed to help me, see? Yes, of course." Her eyes widened and she almost smiled. "Leggett said we should get a gun and try and frighten Memo. I remember that much. That's what he said. He said we'd try you first, and then go over to Memo's."

"But you don't remember the time?"

She shook her head again and again.

I wondered if it had been Memo who had called me to offer ten thousand dollars. I wondered and wondered some more.

I said: "You do, positively, remember firing the gun? It wasn't a dream?"

"I remember," she said. "I can't forget that no matter how hard I try." She rubbed her forehead with the heel of her hand. "He was just sitting there, looking at me. I just shot him, and he tumbled over. I did it."

I got up and went into the bathroom. I rinsed out the glass in there and had a drink of luke-warm tap water.

I walked back into the other room. Honor was lying down again. The towel wasn't covering much. Landrith saw me looking, and she threw the spread over her sister.

"It's a little late for that," I said.

"Where do we go from here?" asked Landrith.

"How'd you find out about the murder and the pictures?"

"Honor told us, Saturday evening."

"Us?"

She looked away.

"You mean, you and the fancy man? Egan?"

"Yes," she said.

"Do you know this Leggett?"

"No. I don't think so." She was looking at me strangely. Suddenly she stepped up close to me. She kissed me lightly on the cheek, then stepped back. "Thank you," she said.

"For what?"

"Anything and everything."

I made a noise with my mouth. I said: "I'm going out now. I'll take your car. Don't, whatever else you do, try to leave this place. Don't call anyone and don't worry about anything. Just stay here. I'll take care of everything."

It was easy to say.

Honor was snoring from the bed as I left. That was the way I wanted it.

CHAPTER SIXTEEN

THE SUN had settled somewhere deep down in the Pacific by the time I got to the neighborhood of 4211 Melrose. Neon signs began sprinkling themselves against the growing darkness and motorists began turning on their car lights.

It wasn't a pretentious neighborhood. It was old, growing shoddy in its late stages; the city college was nearby, and several hospitals, and it was close enough to the casting agencies to make it a haven for the star-crazy kids from all over the world looking for cheap rent. It was a neighborhood that nurses and internes and would-be stars mingled in together, prowled together, searched together, looking for something that would never be there.

I slowed down as I drove by 4211. It wasn't much, but it kept pace with the other buildings along the street. It was a one-story job, probably a duplex or a triplex, muddy-brown in color, and set high on a mound of weeds and unkempt grass twenty feet above street level. A shattered maple tree leaned indignantly against one side, blocking out the view. There was no driveway leading to a garage. I drove around the block and finally spotted the tan fifty-one Chevvie coupe. It was parked on a side street to the east of 4211, right across from an empty filling station. I drove the Thunderbird into the station, parking it along the east wall. The windows were cracked and broken and a gigantic oil spot covered the paving. A phone booth stood silent guard on the west side.

I walked across the street and looked at the Chevvie. The door was unlocked. I opened the door and there was still enough daylight left for me to read the registration slip curled around the steering post: Neal H. Leggett. Right car. Right man.

I stood there. I wanted a look at his apartment. I had an idea what I would find in there. I thought about how I could get him out of the apartment long enough for me to search it. Leggett was a man in a dirty business; he probably was a man with a great deal of fear, fear of his customers, fear of the police, fear of irate husbands of his models.

I walked back across to the phone booth. I thumbed through the tattered phone directory hanging outside and found his number. I searched through my pockets, locating three dimes and a quarter. I hoped that would be enough.

I put in the first dime and dialed the number.

The phone rang four times, then: "Hello?"

I didn't say anything; I didn't recognize the voice.

He said, again: "Hello!"

The voice still didn't strike a familiar note, and I still didn't say anything. I just stood inside the booth and tried to read all the lewd little sayings a thousand different morons had etched into the sides. The man on the other end of the line was quiet for a long time, then he hung up.

I took out my second dime, dialing the same number.

This time, he got to it on the second ring. He waited a moment, then said a hesitant "Hello."

I maintained my silence.

"Who the hell is this?" he asked.

I waited. He made a dirty remark about my ante-cedants and hung up with a bang. I used my final dime. The phone was picked up in the middle of the first ring this time.

"What kind of a game is this?"

I again remained silent.

He swore at me; he had had a lot of practice at it and knew all the right words. They didn't do anything to me. He slammed down the receiver; it shocked my ear.

I flipped the quarter up into the air, caught it, then put it in the slot. I hoped it would do the trick; it was my last bit of change.

But no one answered. I let the phone ring and ring and ring and I kept watching the corner. I wasn't disappointed; a stubby little figure came churning around the corner, knees high, elbows back, looking for all the world like a dash-man heading for the tape. Friend Leggett was in a hurry. And then suddenly I had a thought: who would he be going to at a time like this, when he was frightened? I decided to forgo the searching of his apartment and tail him.

The combination of the distance and the darkness made it impossible for me to see his face.

He jumped into the Chevvie, slamming the door hard; he left an inch of rubber on the pavement as he skidded around the corner.

I was in the Thunderbird immediately. He was heading west on Melrose. I kept a safe distance behind him. We only went about a dozen blocks, then he suddenly turned north into a side street. I switched off my headlights and turned the corner after him. I could see the Chevvie pulling into a driveway in the next block, so I pulled over and parked. I saw his shadow move up the sidewalk, pause for a moment, and then go through a high cement wall. I thought I knew where I was, but I decided to make sure.

I got out and walked up toward the high wall. I saw the Chevvie crammed into a narrow, gravel-topped space between an old shed with a corrugated-iron roof on it, and the high cement wall. I walked on up to where Leggett had gone in. There was a recession in the wall; a small, glassed-in cubicle stood beside a wooden door. There was no lettering on the door, but a brass plaque, corroded and dulled by age and weather, was imbedded in the cement wall. The plaque read: Baum Pictures, Inc., 1922.

Well.

I went back to the Thunderbird and drove around the block. The high cement wall went all the way around, concealing the old Baum studios within; vague shadows and outlines loomed up higher than the wall, resting like gigantic birds ready to pounce on any unsuspecting intruder. The studios hadn't been used, I recalled, since Harry Baum's death, shortly before World War II.

I shot the Thunderbird back on Melrose and drove to 4211.

It was a duplex. There was a light coming from the apartment on the right; a tired radio baritone was telling about the latest skirmish on the Gaza border.

It wasn't hard to get into Leggett's place. The lock was old, and I made it on the second key. I searched the wall for a switch, found it, and clicked on the lights.

The room was small and boxlike, with a high beamed ceiling. It smelled of dust and a lack of clean air. An overstuffed sofa was pushed tightly against the wall on my right, a broken spring peering from the middle cushion; a chair matched it on my left, set in front of french windows that looked out on Melrose. Dirty white linen drapes covered the french windows. There was one straight-backed wooden chair tucked away near an old, battered dresser in the corner near the sofa. A wall bed took up the far wall, one of its brass legs dangling uselessly from its moorings. There was no rug on the floor. A closed door with a glass knob was next to the bed; another door with no knob, and slightly open, led off to the right.

It wasn't much of a place for a guy with Leggett's ideas. Maybe this was his first push; I didn't know.

I tried the door on the right first, and found it led into the kitchen. There was a table with a dirty oilcloth covering, three chairs around the table, a four-burner gas stove, and a refrigerator. I just stood there and looked and thought and then went back into the front room.

I tried the other door. It led into the bathroom. I found the usual shaving gear, toothbrush, toothpaste, aspirin, and a couple of soiled towels. Not what I was looking for.

I went back into the front room and sat down on the broken sofa. I lit a cigarette and looked at the dirty walls. I thought.

I got up and went over to the dresser. The bottom drawer was empty. The middle drawer contained soiled socks, underwear, and shirts. The top drawer contained clean socks, underwear, and shirts. Still not what I wanted. I went over and pulled down the wall bed. In the niche behind the bed was a small closet space, with a raincoat and a light brown gabardine suit hanging neatly from hangers. I went through all the pockets, finding nothing more than match covers. I took the blankets and sheets off the bed; I tore off the pillow slips and ripped apart the pillows. Nothing.

I wasn't getting very far very fast.

I sat down and had another cigarette and thought some more.

I got up and went back into the kitchen. I looked in the oven of the stove. Empty. I leaned up against the refrigerator and wondered if I had been wrong: it had happened before in my life.

And then I saw something: the cord for the refrigerator hung loose out of the socket. I felt the refrigerator; it was warm, and it wasn't vibrating.

I opened the refrigerator door. It was empty inside, empty and warm. I opened the little door at the top where the ice trays usually fit: and I hadn't been wrong after all. There was a cardboard shoebox inside. I took it out and went over to the table and sat down with it.

I took off the top, and saw it was a filing system, little cards, neatly typed, in alphabetical order. There was a name and a phone number on each card, then below that a brief sentence of explanation, such as prefers this kind of girl or that kind of girl; or more than one girl; or blondes only; that sort of thing. Mr. Neal H. Leggett was thorough and businesslike in his approach to the whole thing.

I went through the cards carefully. I recognized two of the names: a city councilman, a female movie star who had been in the top ten box-office poll for six straight years. Leggett operated in a big manner, despite this crummy flat. I ran across one more name that I recognized; it surprised me: and then, all of a sudden, it wasn't surprise after all. I should have figured it that way, after the studio and all. Joel Pendleton—another queer twist in a queer family.

At the back of the shoebox was a smaller box, the kind typewriter ribbons come in. I opened that, and found the negatives. I held them up to the light: the girl in the negatives was Honor Pendleton.

That was good enough for me.

I took the shoebox and its contents and left. I didn't bother turning off the lights.

CHAPTER SEVENTEEN

It was fully dark outside. I took my time driving the short distance back to the Baum studios. I was in no hurry. I had most of it now. But one thing still bothered me … Why Jean Gibbon? That, I couldn't figure; not fully. But I knew I was on the right track.

I parked across the street from the studios. I tried all of my keys in the door but none would fit. I looked up at that high cement wall and decided I was no athlete. I walked up to the corner and back again. There had to be a way into the place.

The Chevvie was still parked between the old shed and the wall. I gauged the distance and decided that I could make it. The Chevvie was parked close enough to the wall for me to climb on the fender and reach the top of the wall with my fingers; I took a deep breath, a good grip, and hauled myself up and over. I dropped down on the other side, falling in the process, stinging the bottoms of my feet.

I sat there and rubbed some life back into my ankles. I got up and looked around for a light somewhere, but couldn't see any. Where was he? Where were *they*? It seemed to be much darker inside the wall than outside; I felt as if I were in a tunnel. I put my right hand out against the wall and, using that for a guide, started to make a swing around the entire place, still looking for a light.

I walked slowly. A huge dark shape suddenly loomed up in front of me; my stomach did a couple of flips, but the thing turned out to be just the model of an old airplane out of some ancient picture about World War I.

I moved around it, kept going among more dark shapes of old picture props. Finally I did spot a light. I walked across the lot toward it, and found that it was coming from a small cottage tucked away between two gigantic sound stages. The cottage was painted white, set behind a well-cared-for, though small, lawn; it probably had been used in the distant past by a big-name movie star. Three steps led up to a veranda with an old-fashioned porch swing on it. A door was at the right, and a wide window covered most of the left side of the front. It was from the window that the light was coming, but I couldn't see inside; green drapes had been drawn across the glass, drapes not thick enough to quite block out the light.

I took a quick look at the left side of the cottage; no light showed there. I went around to the right side; light streamed out, revealing a narrow passageway between the cottage and the sound stage. I squeezed through, ducked under the window from which the light was coming, cautiously lifted my head and looked inside.

The room was well-furnished and tidy. The far wall was done in chocolate-brown, and there also seemed to be a number of paintings or photographs spaced along it, but I couldn't quite make them out. A foam-rubber sofa with wrought-iron legs was against the wall on my right; a man was lying on it, his feet towards me. I couldn't make out his face, but, from his build, I judged him to be Leggett. Two modern Swedish chairs were at the left. I could see the top of a blue yachting cap poking above one of the chairs, and a man's feet were sticking out in front of it, resting on an ottoman. The man's hand was dropped over the arm of the chair, the fingers working themselves gently and persistently into the smooth, thick hair of the Russian wolfhound lying there. But I couldn't see the face. I didn't have to.

The dog raised its head suddenly, looking in the direction of the window behind which I stood; I ducked farther into the shadows, and held my breath for as long as possible. The man's hand crept along and patted the dog's head.

The man on the sofa suddenly got to his feet. His fists were clenched, and he said something I couldn't hear. It was Neal H. Leggett, and I recognized him. He was still five-feet-two with eyes-of-blue; he hadn't changed much since I had seen him Saturday night at the fights. He was still angry at the world. He kept jabbing out with his left arm, his face contorted in temper but, though I strained my ears, I couldn't hear what he was saying. He suddenly took off his coat and threw it down on the sofa. The man in the blue yachting cap hadn't moved, other than to keep his hand running up and down on the dog.

The dog continued to look at the window. I felt a little shiver of fright run through me. The dog suddenly bounded to his feet and bared his teeth. Leggett stopped his talking and swung around to follow the dog's stare. The blue yachting cap moved, and Joel Pendleton stood upright. He looked down at the dog, then out at the window.

I decided it was time to get the hell out of there.

I headed for the back of the house, wanting to stay out of the light as much as possible. My shoulders scraped against the walls on either side of me. I heard the dog's bark from the front of the house—they had let him out. Again that little shiver of fright went through me.

And then I ran right smack into the high cement wall. I tried to turn right or left, but it was useless. I was trapped, backed into a hole with no way out except past that damned dog. Both the cottage and the sound stage were butted up against the wall, with no back entrances.

I had been a fool. I didn't even have a gun on me. At that moment, I would have given ten years of my life for a gun, any gun.

I could hear the dog padding down the narrow space toward me. The animal wasn't hurrying; it had all the time in the world, and it seemed to realize this. A deep, low-down growl reached my ears. I placed my shoulders back up against the wall and yelled: "Call him off. I'm coming out."

Someone laughed from the front of the cottage; it wasn't quite a human laugh.

The dog crouched low before me, settling on its haunches, ready to spring. The growling was constant, and I sweated with fear. And then a voice yelled: "All right, Turk. Here, Turk."

The dog waited for a fraction of a moment, and I waited, too. And then it started inching backward, growling and keeping those huge teeth bared for my benefit.

I took a big breath, and slowly followed the dog. I was as close to it as I ever wanted to be.

Joel Pendleton stood near the corner of the veranda, on the grass, the light from the open door playing tricks with his face. I thought he was laughing, but I couldn't be sure. Leggett was on the veranda, leaning over the railing. He watched me carefully as I walked out and stood in the light. The dog stayed about a yard away from me, giving me hungry, dissatisfied looks.

Leggett's voice whined against the sudden stillness. "Jesus," he said, "it's that private eye. Phelan."

"I've seen you before," said Joel Pendleton.

I didn't say one word. I just stood there and kept staring down at that dog. I didn't want him at my throat. He looked as big as a horse.

Joel Pendleton said, "I think we'd all better go inside and have a little talk."

I didn't argue with him.

We went inside, the three of us, and the dog. The dog seemed aware of its power to frighten me, seemed to enjoy doing so.

Joel Pendleton passed me to go into a darkened back room; he returned with a kitchen stool, placing it in a corner of the room, near the chocolate-brown wall. He told me to sit on it. I did. The dog lay down on the gray carpet in front of me, still eying me hungrily; maybe they hadn't fed him that day.

Joel Pendleton sat down in the chair he had occupied before. He pushed the blue yachting cap to the back of his head and crossed his legs. He had a long, thin nose that drooped down over an almost chinless lower face. His lips were wide and flat and unnaturally red. He was apparently quite at ease.

I wasn't.

Leggett wandered around the room, obviously upset and nervous.

"Well, Mr. Phelan—is that right?—" I nodded, and he continued, "—let's have our little talk."

"About what?"

"Let's begin with what you are doing here. You're trespassing on private property."

"I was taking a walk," I said. Blood was pumping back into my veins.

Pendleton laughed. It was that same laugh I had heard earlier, still not quite human.

I chanced a look up at the wall. It was covered with oil paintings and photographs. Everything from tiny postcard-sized things to a gigantic oil painting, about five-by-seven-feet. The girl in the painting had her head turned away, but not her breasts.

"Nice," Pendleton said, "isn't it?"

"I don't know. I don't go in for that sort of thing."

"You have only yourself to blame."

Leggett continued to move around the room. The dog shifted its gaze one time from me to consider Leggett; the latter shuddered at that. I didn't blame him.

"He might have a gun on him, Mr. Pendleton," said Leggett.

Pendleton smiled a bit. "You are a fool, Leggett. If he had had a gun, he would have used it out there."

"Just the same, I'd better search him."

"That won't be necessary." Again Pendleton smiled a bit. "It would be interesting, if he did have a gun, to see him try and reach it. Very interesting. Turk moves almost with the speed of light."

My mouth was dry, but I said: "I'm not much of a gun-toter."

Leggett walked between the dog and me. I thought, briefly, of pushing him into the mutt and making a try for the door. But that's all I did, think about it. I've seen Russian wolfhounds run. They're almost as fast as greyhounds.

"Again," said Pendleton, "I'll ask you what you are doing here, Mr. Phelan."

"I'm trying to solve a murder," I said. "A murder that your kid sister thinks she committed."

Something flickered in the backs of Pendleton's eyes. He studied his hands, bending his head forward.

"That is interesting," he said. "Leggett here seems to know you quite well. I believe that I saw you at my mother's house last Sunday."

"You did."

"And you are a private investigator?"

"That's right."

"Just whom are you working for, and why?"

"For your father, because someone was blackmailing your mother with photos of your sister, Honor."

"You'll have to excuse my ignorance, Mr. Phelan. I have as little to do with my family as possible. I'm not up on all these matters." He paused, lifting his head to stare at Leggett. "You say my sister *thinks* she killed someone? Doesn't she know?"

"She knows she pulled a trigger and shot someone."

"I don't understand you."

"I'll make it simple, if you like. As I said, your father hired me to get back the negatives of the photos of your sister. You know Memo Sanchez?" He nodded slightly. "He started the game. At least, I think he did, but it doesn't matter now, one way or the other. Memo was killed Saturday. Honor told me just a short time ago that she was the one who killed him. I don't believe she did. She sincerely thinks she did, though, which complicates matters. She was drunk, you probably know how drunk she can get. She wasn't quite sure of everything that happened. She did fire a shot into Memo; that's true enough. The shot was heard around six o'clock Saturday evening. But Memo was actually killed some three hours earlier than that. You see, he had been dead for some time, and the guy who planned the whole thing knew this. He also knew your sister's drinking habits, her way of not ever being sure of what she was doing or where she was while she was drinking."

"Interesting," said Joel Pendleton. "Tell me more."

"The actual murderer was almost too smart for his own good. He quarreled with Memo, over what I'm not sure; probably the amount of the blackmail. He made it look as if he was siding with Honor when she found out about the blackmailing. He made it sound good. He was going to help her get back the negatives and the photos and take care of Mr. Sanchez. He helped her, all right. He took her out and got her good and drunk and had her go up to your other sister's apartment and pick up a gun. Then, he ducked away for a while, shot and killed Memo with that gun, and returned to her. He again got her drunk, drunk enough so she wouldn't be aware of everything that was going on. He whispered in her little old ear that the only way out was for her to kill Memo. She bit on that. He took her back up to Memo's apartment and let her shoot a dead man. It took a little guts, going up there the second time, but it was worth the risk. Now, he had the negatives and he also had a murder-rap hanging over her. He could really twist the screw now." I looked at Leggett. "Couldn't be, Leggett?"

Leggett licked at dry lips, said nothing.

Pendleton moved a little in the chair, uncrossing his legs.

I had put the small box in my pocket, the box with the negatives in it. I started to put my hand in my pocket, and the dog rose to its feet, growling. I held my hand outside, straight in front of me, looking at Pendleton.

I said, "I've got something to show you. It's in my pocket."

He didn't hesitate, "All right, Turk."

I took out the box and tossed it across the short space to Pendleton. He opened it, studying the negatives against the light. He nodded while looking at them.

I said: "I found those in Leggett's apartment, not an hour ago. He pulled a real dumb play today. He got your sister all tanked up again and brought her around to my apartment. Something happened to make him change his mind about blackmailing her for the murder. Maybe he got cold feet; maybe something else, I don't know. But he brought her around and told her to kill me. He fed her a line about my having been in cahoots with Sanchez. He knew I'd get that gun away from her. I was no sitting target. He also knew I'd check the gun with the police, which is just what I did. He figured she'd blurt out her confession, which she did. But he made the mistake of not knowing that I knew Honor had shot a man already dead."

"Who was it that heard the second shot?" asked Pendleton.

"That doesn't matter," I said. "Not now."

I looked up at that wall again.

"It might," he said. "Is she around?"

I didn't answer that.

"He's screwy, Mr. Pendleton," Leggett said. "Jesus, why would I do all that? I don't need the dough."

"Your kind always needs the dough, Leggett," I said. "You killed Sanchez Saturday afternoon, then called me up and rigged that meeting at the fights. But you got scared and didn't go through with the rest of it. You lack guts, Leggett. You make me sick."

"This witness that heard the shot," said Pendleton. "I'm interested in her."

"Why? She's dead. Also murdered."

Pendleton's eyebrows rose. He stared at Leggett with hatred.

Leggett moved closer to the sofa. I had an idea what he was going to do, but I didn't interfere. I let him do it. He grabbed up his coat from the sofa, and the gun jerked out in his hand. The dog growled, shifting attention from me. Leggett backed toward the door.

"Why did you, Leggett?" asked Pendleton, not moving. "You said you just wanted to take more pictures."

"Ah, you sonofabitch," said Leggett. "You rich, nogood, perverted sonofabitch. I had it figured. I had it."

"Turk," said Pendleton.

The dog was a long gray line moving in the air. Leggett fired, missing. I heard the bullet smack into the wall above my head. The dog's teeth closed in around Leggett's throat. Man and dog went down in a rolling, jumping heap. Leggett fired again, uselessly, the bullet going into the ceiling. The gun fell from his grasp. The dog had a good hold now, shaking Leggett's head like a man wringing a chicken's neck. I jumped down from the stool and picked up the gun. Leggett's screams were slowly dying out; he locked his arms around the dog's midsection, squeezing. I couldn't get it a good shot. It was horrible: a rolling ball of screams and growls, blood and wool. Finally, the dog's head reared up for a fraction of a second. That was all I needed. I fired. The bullet smashed its head, twirling the body around; I fired again. The dog's body jumped a little; the dog whimpered sadly, then again, then was still.

I stooped over Leggett. There wasn't any use. The dog's teeth had ripped apart his jugular vein; the blood was pumping out, slower and slower. His face was a mass of teeth marks and claw scratches. I felt like vomiting. I've seen death in many, many ways, but never like that.

I turned back to Pendleton. He was stooped over the dog. He was crying.

CHAPTER EIGHTEEN

I SAT quite still, my hands folded quietly on the formica-topped kitchen table. The table was a basic yellow, with a mass of red semi-circles running through it; the semicircles were small and pencil-thin, and all ran into each other. It was all very confusing. I tried to follow one line of red all the way across the table top; I failed. I tried again; again I failed.

I could hear the sound of voices coming from the other room. Police voices; efficient voices; dry, everyday voices. I had called them. Lundeberg and Wheeler and a mass of technicians had arrived. I was in the kitchen, the light from above too bright for my weary eyes, my only company a uniformed cop. He cleared his throat uncomfortably, and I turned to look at him. He was leaning with his back braced against the wall. He was young, tall, heavily built; he had over-hanging eyebrows and a jutting jaw. His blue eyes were icy cold and uncompromising: he was Dan Lundeberg or Adam Wheeler twenty years ago.

I asked, surprised at my own voice: "What time is it?"

"Why?"

"I just wondered."

"Well, quit wondering. You're not going nowhere."

"No," I said. "I guess I'm not."

He grinned in a self-satisfied manner; he was happy with himself. He'd go home after this was all over and he'd tell some cute little wench about all the nuts he had seen that night on duty and then he'd take that cute little wench to bed with him and blame the rest of the world for being the way it was; nothing was wrong with him.

To hell with him.

He started to say something, then stopped. The kitchen door swung open beside him. Dan Lundeberg stood in the doorway, looking in at me; he looked a long time, and there was one helluva lot in the look. The sound of the voices from the other room increased. I could see past Lundeberg, into the other room. Two bored-looking men in heavily starched white doctor's smocks were just picking up Leggett's body; they weren't very careful as they dropped it on a stretcher. I guess Leggett didn't mind. A flash bulb popped somewhere off to the side, giving the room an unreal, ghastly look for one brief second. The two bored-looking men each took one end of the stretcher; they picked it up and carted the body out of my sight. Adam Wheeler crossed behind Lundeberg. He didn't look in at me; I didn't blame him. Lundeberg shook his head at me, then closed the door, remaining in the other room.

I tried the game with the red lines again; for the third time, I lost.

The minutes dragged by. Time was nothing; it slowed, and then slowed some more. But, as the young cop had said, I was going nowhere.

The young cop kept his silence and so did I, and then, finally, the kitchen door swung open again and Lundeberg and Wheeler came into the kitchen. Lundeberg walked up to the table; he hunched his shoulders forward and looked down at his hands. Wheeler spoke to the young cop in a low tone; the young cop saluted smartly, and left.

Lundeberg said: "Stand up."

I did.

I knew what was coming, but I let him have his fun; I owed him that much, maybe even more. I had cut too many corners; this I knew.

He doubled up his right fist and swung. The blow caught me on my upper lip. I felt myself falling back-succeeded in bringing a chair down with me. Things wards; I reached out, trying to catch myself, and only darkened briefly; Lundeberg's face above me changed colors, and then became light again. He could punch. He could do that. I brought a hand up, wiping at my mouth. Blood showed against my hand; my blood. I spit on the floor, and swallowed some blood.

Lundeberg said: "The last time I hit anyone like that was over six years ago. He was a young punk with a sassy mouth and a gripe against the world. He had raped some middle-aged woman out on Wilshire some place. I beat hell out of him, just because he sassed me." He paused; he was breathing heavily, and his facial muscles were working overtime. He took out a cigarette, holding it loosely in his right hand, studying the knuckles of that hand. "You gripe me in the same way, Phelan." He laughed. "Police brutality. I'm a great big brute…" He laughed again.

I didn't say anything.

He said, "You deserved that, and maybe a lot more. I remember the old days, Phelan. We used to work over guys like you. Sometimes, I wish the public minded its own goddamned business and didn't interfere with mine."

"Take it easy, Dan," said Wheeler.

Lundeberg didn't look at him; he just looked down at me. "Get up," he said.

I got up. Lundeberg studied the cigarette in his right hand, and nodded his head. I picked up the chair, setting it upright by the table. My mouth had ceased its bleeding. I took out my handkerchief and wiped away blood. I didn't look at either one of them.

"It was nice of you to call us," Lundeberg said. "Damned nice of you. Almost too damned nice. I suppose you want a pat on the back now. You think you're a great big goddamned hero now, don't you? I think you stink, Phelan. I could book you. I could book you and throw away the book. I could have your license, too. I might yet; I haven't made up my mind. You've caused me a lot of trouble." He jerked his hand in Wheeler's direction. "Wheeler's butt is way down deep in a hole. You two are supposed to be friends, guys that spent a lot of time in the dirt together during the war. Hell, you've thrown the dirt right in his face, Phelan. You didn't even give him a fair shake, and he went to bat for you. He's got a wife and kids, but I don't let that bother me none. I don't like what he did. His loyalty was in the wrong place. He's in my department, and I don't like guys in my department doing favors for smart guys like you. No, I don't. I could have his badge, could have him thrown off the force for doing what he did." He turned slightly, staring at Wheeler. "I don't know. I might do that yet, too."

"Don't take it out on him," I said.

"Don't tell me what to do, Phelan. Just keep your goddamned mouth shut for awhile. Let me cool down. Just do that."

I let him do that.

The silence grew for three, four minutes; then, finally, Lundeberg stuck the cigarete in his mouth and lit it.

He said: "Sit down."

I sat down.

"Now talk. I want the whole thing, from beginning to end. If you leave out anything, no matter how small, I'll hang you by your thumbs."

I talked. I began at the beginning, as he wanted, and went through the whole thing. I told him about J. Walter Pendleton coming to see me; I told him about the phone call and the offer to sell the negatives for $10,000; I told him about the night in the Dorsett jail; I told him about what Jean Gibbon had said, that she had heard the shot at about six o'clock; I told him about the Pendleton sisters; I told him about finding the negatives and the filing system at Leggett's apartment; I told him everything but one thing: and that was far too personal to tell him; he probably wouldn't have been interested anyway.

I talked for a long time. My throat got dry and parched, but no one seemed to mind that. After I finished, I got up and went over and had a drink of water from the faucet.

The two of them just stood there, each with his own thoughts. Lundeberg had smoked through three cigarettes; Wheeler hadn't done anything but look at me.

Finally, Lundeberg moved. He went over to the door, opened it slightly, said something to someone in the other room, then closed the door, turning back to me.

"It all adds up," said Lundeberg. "If fits. We knew the Gibbon girl was holding back on us. People always got to hold back something; they never realize it costs them in the end. They never do."

"You're jumping the gun," I said.

He raised his eyes to stare at me, then shook his head. "Our medical examiner gave us the information about Sanchez being shot a few hours after death. Apparently, Leggett didn't know we could tell that. He wasn't very bright."

"He got scared," I said. "That's all. He got greedy, wanting double blackmail, then he got scared. He was a little man with big ideas, too big for him. It cost him."

"Yeah," said Lundeberg. "That it did."

"I guess he had time to think about the whole thing over the weekend, and decided to dump the whole thing in Honor Pendleton's lap. He figured I'd get the gun from her and have it checked. He figured she'd confess. What about her?"

Lundeberg shrugged. "We'll have to pick her up. There'll be a technical charge of some kind. The mere fact that she fired the gun *thinking* she killed someone makes her a criminal—I believe. I'm not familiar with the legal side of that. The D.A.'ll have to worry about that."

"She's a sick kid. She needs help."

"That's not my department, Phelan. I'm a cop, not a psychiatrist. Just a cop, nothing more."

"Yeah," I said. "Nothing more."

The door opened and the young cop came in, bringing the shoebox with Leggett's filing system in it. He handed the box to Lundeberg, then left again. Lundeberg sat down at the table, going through the cards. He shook his head a couple of times. When he had finished, he looked up at me.

"The press would like to get hold of some of these," he said. "Some big names here."

"Pretty big," I said.

"Did you take anything out of here?"

"The negatives of Honor Pendleton. I gave them to her brother."

"Anything else?"

"One of the cards."

"Whose name was on it?"

I told him. He looked surprised.

"Anything else on the card?"

"Look for yourself," I said, handing him the card.

He read it at least four times and then looked up at the ceiling, almost as if he expected to find an answer up there to his question.

"This smears the picture," he said. "Goddamn."

I said: "You saw those typewritten letters in Jean Gibbon's apartment. I don't figure Leggett murdered her, too. He didn't know she had heard the second shot. Someone else murdered her; someone with a far different motive."

"Goddamn," Lundeberg said again.

Wheeler walked over to the table. He picked up the card, reading it. He shifted his gaze to my face. I didn't look at him.

"We had him and let him go," said Wheeler.

"That wasn't very bright," I said.

Lundeberg swore; he swore a long time. "It's not our case anyway. She was murdered at Malibu; that's county territory. Let the sheriff worry about it." He was only kidding himself; not me. He swung a fist down on the table top, jarring the whole table.

"How in hell were we supposed to know this, Phelan? You had it all tucked away. We couldn't hold him. He gave a statement, and that was that."

"Okay," I said. "I'm not arguing with you. There's no real evidence. We could probably match up the typewriting on those letters with a typewriter somewhere. I don't know. But someone must have seen him leave the Red Barn with Jean Gibbon Saturday night. We can check that."

"Goddamn," Lundeberg said again.

Lundeberg got to his feet. Wheeler and I followed him into the other room. The dog still lay where it had fallen after I had shot it; it looked just as mean dead as it had alive. I still remembered my fright. A huge dark circle had darkened the rug. Leggett's blood; and the dog's.

"Okay if I use the phone?"

Lundeberg nodded, not looking at me.

I went over to the phone and picked it up. I dialed a number. The guy who had been in *Birth of a Nation* didn't like my calling him at that time of the night, but he had my information. It wasn't conclusive, but it was enough to go on. I could add it up.

I hung up the phone and turned around to Lundeberg. He was standing in front of the chocolate-covered wall, staring up at all the photographs and the paintings; he was shaking his head.

"I got two teen-age daughters," he said. "Stuff like this makes me sick. My stomach does a flip. I'd hate to think of one of 'em going out with some guys that go in for this type of thing."

"They're sick," I said. "Mentally sick."

"I guess so," he said.

"I know where Honor Pendleton is," I said. "Maybe the other guy, too."

Lundeberg swung around to stare at me. "You're a bright sonofabitch, Phelan," he said. "Goddamn you. Get out of here. Take a boat to China. I don't wanna ever see your stinking face again. It annoys me."

I started to leave.

"Take Wheeler with you. You two are such buddy-buddies. Go on outside and laugh at me. Go on."

He was as hard as a rock. Sure.

CHAPTER NINETEEN

We took the Thunderbird. We drove in silence. There didn't seem to be much to say between us. Wheeler huddled against the far door, not looking at me, his mouth working hard over a piece of gum. I knew it was inside him, just like it was inside me. But things weren't wrapped up; not yet. I had used our friendship, a friendship based on life-and-death sharings in past times; for that, I was ashamed. I couldn't bring myself to say anything about it. It gnawed inside me, and I let it.

We drove by the motel and stopped. The two Pendleton sisters weren't around; I hadn't figured they would be. The clan was gathering. They had probably left soon after I had earlier in the evening.

We took the long drive out to the Pendleton estate. Ventura Boulevard shot through the San Fernando Valley. The shops were closed. A few night prowlers were on their way home to wait for another night and another chance. It was strange, strange and cool.

Dawn was just breaking across a bleak sky as we drove up past the rolling lawn and stopped in front of the Pendleton estate. A dark-faced little Jap was busily clipping a hedge; his shears made a sharp clicking noise in the otherwise still morning.

We got out of the car and stood before the door. Wheeler whistled silently between his teeth.

"Some layout," he said.

"It's how the upper one percent lives," I said.

"Let 'em," he said. "To hell with 'em all, Johnny." He grinned a big grin. "They got their problems, just like we have."

"Yeah," I said. "I'm sorry about everything, Adam. I almost pulled the chain on you."

"You did," he said, "but forget it. I do what I want to do, and that's all. Lundeberg talks big, but I know him. His heart's as soft as marshmallow. He won't do anything to me about this. He talks big."

I gripped him on the shoulder. That was that.

I rang the bell, and we waited. It was finally opened by Landrith Pendleton. She hadn't changed clothes; she looked as if she hadn't been to bed yet.

"You're early," she said.

"Not early enough," I said.

"We're all here. Come on in."

We followed her into the house and down that long hallway, turning into the room in which I had talked with Mrs. Pendleton on Sunday. There were a lot of people in the room for that time of morning. I got the idea we had interrupted something, and I thought I knew what that something was.

Big, handsome Richie Egan was standing before the windows, looking outside. He turned, briefly, to stare at us. I was not surprised to see him. His mouth was thin and uncompromising. Mrs. Pendleton was in that wicker rocking chair, the same blanket over her legs; she had her eyes closed and was humming to herself. Honor Pendleton sat on the floor, her head resting against her mother's knees; she seemed to be asleep.

I said: "This is Lieutenant Wheeler of the L.A. police force. He's here on official business."

"You didn't waste any time, did you?" asked Landrith.

"It's not what you think," I said.

Egan whirled around. He raised his right arm up in the air, staring at me. He said: "You got a funny way of working for a client, shamus."

I said, "I'm not in the mood to take anything from any of you. I did a lot for this screwed-up family, more than I should have done. You don't deserve it, none of you. I don't know what'll happen to Honor; that's out of my hands. She's a sick girl. She needs psychiatric help. She didn't kill Sanchez, though she thinks she did." Honor opened her eyes, looking at me. "Leggett killed Sanchez, then rigged it to make her think she did the job. All she did was pull the trigger and shoot a dead man. But she did a lot of other things, things that are sickening, things that all the money in the world can't correct. She's got to pay for doing what she did."

Egan said: "Is that right? About Leggett killing Sanchez?"

"Yeah," Wheeler said. "That's right."

"Of course, it's right," I said. "But you haven't been right with me, Egan, not by a long shot."

"That's too goddamned bad," he said.

"Don't get tough," I said. "Don't try it. We're not in Dorsett now. You don't have that phoney sheriff or any of your muscle-boys with you. You try anything now, and I'll kick your teeth down your throat."

Egan took a step toward me, his fists clenched tightly. I waited for him. I wanted him to come on, but he didn't.

I said: "This whole family is rotten to the core. It stinks to high heaven. It's got most of the money in this world, but none of the morals nor the guts. It just plain stinks. You came out here from the east a long time ago, Egan. You were a bright boy. You got mixed up with a young girl with a lot of dough behind her; she got pregnant and had a kid, and then you suddenly had some of that dough. You've had it ever since, haven't you?"

Egan's shoulders slumped sadly. He backed up.

Landrith said: "No, please."

"It's not what you think, Mr. Phelan." Mrs. Pendleton said this, her voice low and cutting. "It's not what you think at all."

"How would you know what I think?" I asked. "You're no better than the rest of them, Mrs. Pendleton."

"I know that," she said, quietly. "Mr. Phelan, I know that. Just wait a minute and listen to me. Don't blame Richie, Mr. Phelan. Don't blame him."

She lifted her eyes to share a glance with Egan; there was something almost tender between them at that moment.

"I want Honor to hear this, too. Lannie knows about it; she's the only one that does in the family. I told her a long time ago. Maybe I should've told Joel and Honor then, too, but I didn't have the nerve. Lannie was always so strong and the other two so weak. It's true what you said, Mr. Phelan, or intimated. I was married to Walter, had just been married to him, but it was no marriage in the strict sense. There was nothing between us. To this day, our marriage has not been consummated. Funny, isn't it? My father knew; he knew everything, damn his soul in hell. I was his only child, and he wanted the dynasty he had created to live after him, so he demanded I have children. He—he *hired* Richie to furnish the manpower. But the funny thing was that Richie and I fell in love."

"We've been in love all these years, but we've never done anything about it in front of the world," Egan said bitterly.

"Instead," she resumed, "we've sneaked around, had our love in little places and in short times. It sounds sordid, maybe, to you, but it was our lives. We didn't mean to harm anyone. I've hidden behind a false illness for so long that, I don't know, maybe I really am sick now. It would serve me right. Richie is the father of all my children, Mr. Phelan. He's been a good father to Lannie; she's known about him. Joel and Honor didn't know; they turned into weaklings and, for that, I blame myself, and no one else. I gave Lannie a father with which to strengthen herself; I gave nothing to the other two children other than money and complete freedom. You've seen the results. Don't blame them; blame me."

"It may be a little worse than you think," I said.

"What do you mean?" asked Mrs. Pendleton.

"Ask Egan," I said. "He knows."

"I don't know anything, man," said Egan.

Mrs. Pendleton shook her head from side to side. She didn't understand what was going on. Wheeler walked across the room; he helped Honor to her feet. The girl stood there, looking quiet and dumb, trying to grasp a lifetime in a few short minutes.

Egan crossed to stand beside Mrs. Pendleton. He carressed her gently on the shoulder; their love seemed genuine. It was a touching scene: it was, if you didn't know all the filth and all the undercurrents that had gone into bringing them where they were.

"Where's Joel now?" I asked.

"He's in his room," said Egan.

"Do you get him, or do I?"

"Why?" asked Mrs. Pendleton. "What in the world has Joel to do with all this?"

"He's the sickest one of the bunch," I said.

Her eyes widened; she looked at me, and then up at Egan, and then down at the floor. Something like a shudder ran through her frail body.

"You tell her, Egan," I said. "He's your son."

"What did you want me to do?" said Egan. "Turn in my own boy?" His facial muscles twitched unnaturally. "Sure, I know what happened. One of the girls saw him at the Barn, Sunday night—saw him leave with that Jean Gibbon. Hell, I didn't plan it that way. I had you put in jail that night because I figured you for a smart shamus, Phelan, a guy who would dig deep. I wanted to protect Honor, that's all. I figured she had killed Sanchez. But in protecting her, I leave the door open, and my son kills someone else. A nice twist!"

Mrs. Pendleton gasped; the noise seemed to shock everyone in the room for a long minute.

"A nice twist, Egan," I said, finally, "but not quite the right one. Your daughter didn't kill anyone, and neither did your son." I watched his face. It blanched a couple of shades lighter. "Joel had an unhealthy attachment for Jean Gibbon. He wrote her notes, notes of adoration, but he never had the nerve to face her, not until Sunday night, and then he was forced into doing it, forced to do it by something even greater than his adoration of the girl: fear, fear for his life, and the way he led it. That photographer, Leggett, was a very thorough man in his business, almost too thorough. He found out, somehow, in some way, that Jean had heard the second shot that Saturday night, the one that Honor fired. He knew it was only a matter of time until the police put it together; he had to get rid of the one person who had heard the second shot. And he used Joel to do this; he blackmailed Joel into going to the Barn and luring Jean outside. I don't know for sure how Joel managed to do it, but do it he did. Maybe he told her the truth, that he was the one who had been sending her all those letters; I'm not sure. But Leggett thought he was in the clear. No one would see him with the girl, and he had this blackmail thing to hang over Joel's head. Only, in the end, it backfired, and Mr. Leggett got his from a vicious killer-dog. He murdered Jean, just as he had murdered Sanchez before, and he made it look like a passion-killing so that, if it ever came up in the future, he could use his sordid knowledge against Joel and pin the murder on him. It's filthy; the whole thing stinks."

No one said anything. We all were thinking hard, letting the thing pile up and sort itself out.

The gunshot shocked us all.

I took a deep breath, and shook my head. I hadn't counted on that.

Egan led the way, with Wheeler and I following. I knew there was no use hurrying. We crossed that room with all the Louis XIV furnishings in it, and went up another hallway to a door at the far end. Egan opened the door, and went inside; Wheeler followed him. I waited a moment, then went in.

Joel Pendleton lay on the floor, his body crumpled at a sharp angle, a pool of blood forming on the rug near his head, a gun lying on the floor near his outstretched right hand. Wheeler had bent down over him. Wheeler looked up at me, shaking his head. I turned to watch Egan. Nothing showed on his face for a long while.

And then, Egan said: "He always took the easy way out of things. He didn't know any better."

I let it go at that.

There was a photograph of Jean in a nice gold frame on the desk in the corner. I crossed over and picked it up, studying it for some moments; then, I turned, looking down at the dead man on the floor: maybe we'd both been a little nuts over her; maybe.

I took the photograph out of the frame and ripped it apart. That much I could do for her.

The hell with them, I thought; the hell with them all.

I rapped lightly on the door, staring at the blue star right in the middle of it. No one answered from the other side, so I tried the knob; it was unlocked, and I went inside.

J. Walter Pendleton was lying in the middle of the floor, his feet crossed on the second rung of the kitchen stool. He turned his head slightly to look at me, but didn't bother to get up.

"Really, Mr. Phelan," he said, "this is the second time you've disturbed me. I don't like it."

"Your wife told me you were in here," I said. "I just thought you'd like to know everything has been settled."

"Well," he said, rubbing the back of his head against the floor, "I'm happy to hear that. I congratulate you on your fine work."

I hesitated, looking around at the white walls, each with its little blue star.

"How's the work going, Mr. Pendleton?"

"Fine," he said, enthused. "I've really got it this time, Mr. Phelan. My latest creation will shock the world, believe me."

I did; I believed him.

"A little matter is pending, Mr. Pendleton," I said. "My fee."

"How much? After all, you accomplished very little. You did get the negatives, but—"

"I'll leave it to you," I said. This was the guy I had turned down ten thousand dollars for, twice.

He sniffed, found his billfold somewhere in his clothes, handed me a crisp hundred-dollar bill.

"Gee, thanks," I said.

He looked at the door, and I got his meaning. I saluted him on my way out; he was quite a guy. The Pendleton-Egan family was quite a family, what there was left of it.

If that's what money and fame did to you, I was glad I had neither.

I took a cab back to Hollywood. It cost a lot, but it was worth it. I wanted nothing to do with anyone for awhile. I had the cabbie stop once, and I got out and made a phone call with a dime I borrowed from him.

The voice on the other end was still cautious. "Yes?"

"Eddie, this is Phelan."

"How you doing, Johnny?"

"I can't complain. How's it with you?"

"Ah, my wife bought that stove and refrigerator. She's never satisfied."

"Take a bet for me."

"Sure, Johnny-boy."

"A hundred to win on Missie Gloom in the third."

"Ah, Johnny-boy, you're nuts. She won't even get outa the gate."

"Just make the bet."

"It's your money, Johnny. But it won't be for long."

I guess he was right; he usually was.

THE END